BLOw INS

From there to here…

By

Andrew Knowles

While all the stories in this book are true, some names and identifying details have been changed to protect the privacy of the people involved.

For Angie ...

CONTENTS

ACKNOWLEDGEMENTS

This book could not have been written without the help and guidance of Margaret Nohily of Lanesborough, for which, *míle buíochas.*

I am also indebted to the lifelong friendship of Brown and Robert, for just that.

Thanks also to Mr Liam Connerton for help with matters GAA. (All errors, if any, are mine…)

Angie and I would also like to thank our friends on both sides of the Irish Sea, but in particular those in Lanesborough-Ballyleague who have helped us settle into this wonderful community.

Slainte

Why have I written this book? Firstly, because it was great fun, and writing a book was something I had always dreamed of doing. What held me back? Confidence for one, and an inability to plot, the other.

So, what changed?

Well, I was in a shop in the beautiful town of Kilkenny, when for the umpteenth time I was asked, "So what made you move to Ireland?"

A few minutes later, I was in the car driving back home to Co. Longford when a lightbulb came on.

I hope it makes you smile.

PREFACE

"Pull over just up here." She indicates to the left where a man is in his garden. I pull over and she gets out. I hear her say "Excuse me" and then start talking to the man. At first, he looks puzzled, then his face lights up and he starts to point, leaning slightly over, and moving his arm around imaginary corners. He straightens and seems genuinely pleased that he's been able to help. As Ange gets back in the car, he gives us a cheery, smiley wave on our way.

"Turn left in about quarter of a mile," she says.

"So who was that?" I ask, pulling away from the kerb and following her instructions.

"No idea," she replies, "but wasn't he nice!"

I drive on but have to ask; "So you stopped to ask a complete stranger where Pauline lives?"

"Yes," she replied, looking at me like I was stupid. "It was difficult at first because he knew two or three Paulines, but once I'd mentioned Dad's family, he knew exactly who I meant; he even said she'd be at home, because she's on nights this week."

1

PART ONE

CHAPTER 1

Friday/Saturday

IT WAS A DARK AND STORMY NIGHT

It was a dark and stormy night … No, really! It *was* a dark and stormy night.

First dates are always a little trepidatious, they make you a bit edgy and excited at the same time and the really odd thing about this blind date is that, not only was it suggested by my wife, she was coming with me.

I had spent years being told about this beautiful Erin, she would charm me and make me laugh, entice me like a siren, I would be jelly in her hands.

I couldn't wait to meet her.

But first, I had to sit in this Fishguard queue waiting for the overnight ferry.

What a joy a wet West Wales isn't, on a rainy windswept night at one in the morning. The rain sheeting against the windscreen as though thrown from a bucket in some silent movie caper. People were moving around, dressed in Cagoules, and holding barely controllable umbrellas while trying to walk definitely recalcitrant dogs up and down the sides of the parking lanes, all in the vain hope of getting them to do a final poo; then, with so many eyes watching, having little choice but to adopt a Pilates-in-a-wind-tunnel pose to retrieve said stools.

Our two manufacturers of dog poo were in the back, having been well emptied before we reached the port. They just sit there now, barking like lunatics at every other dog they spot.

I turned to Head Office and asked if she'd like a coffee; she would. My turn to brave the West Wales wind and wet. Fortunately, being early birds, we were towards the front of one of the traffic lanes, so my journey to the small café area was not arduous and only a little dampening.

Inside, people sat at canteen tables, nursing hot drinks and stuffing too tired children with chocolate and crisps.

I joined a small queue and slowly arrived in front of one of the least appetising displays of cake, biscuits, and sandwiches it has ever been my pleasure to ignore. I reached the somewhat heavy and blousy serving girl and ordered our drinks; uncharitably, my first thought was back to a bluesy rock band of my youth called Blodwyn Pig, I really did hope this girl wasn't called Blodwyn.

MYSTERY SHOPPER REPORT FORM

1) Were you greeted in a friendly manner? NO

2) Was eye contact made by the staff member? NEARLY

2) Did the staff member smile? NO

4) Were you engaged in a positive manner? NO

5) Having placed your order, were you asked if there was anything else you required? NO

6) Having paid, were you thanked for your custom? NO

7) On leaving the till area, did the staff member trill, "Have a nice day"? GUESS…

I genuinely hoped Blodwyn was on about 75K a year, I'd want that for working in that place for what I guess might only be a four-hour shift, say midnight to 4.00 a.m. Yuk! I'm guessing though that if she were on 75K a year, she would have had far more tattoos, rings, and studs about her generous person than the dozen or so that were on show now.

Back in the car we sat and waited, it would still be a half hour or so before we started to board, so we let the coffees steam up the windows and pretended to nap.

Thirty minutes or so later, a Hi-Vizzed man points to the only car in front of me and we inch forward then seamlessly join the last car exiting the lane to our left. It always seems paradoxical that having kept you waiting for what seemed like an eternity, when they actually get round to loading the boat, they always seem to want to do it in record time. Every fifty yards or so there is another Hi-Viz jacket indicating with a sweep of Hi-Vizzed arm to keep moving.

The sight of all this Hi-Vizzed activity sends Honey, our Golden Retriever into paroxysms' of barking lunacy.

At Fishguard the heavy stuff, lorries, coaches etc. embark through the mouth as it were. The boat opens at the front in a gigantic yawn and swallows the vehicles as though sucking up a string of spaghetti. We cars, on the other hand, have to make a more intricate manoeuvre through a portal which might be described as the ship's ear. This necessitates a near ninety-degree turn off a quite narrow roadway high up the side of the ship and onto the car decks. Lorries orally, cars aurally!

Once on the car deck, more Hi-Vizzes - to the accompaniment of barking dog - park you with the precision of a Swiss watchmaker.

Head office gathers together all that we will need upstairs while I settle the dogs with half a Bonio each and put a small bowl of water in the boot with them. We head for the orange stairs, note that we are Deck Six, Orange, and make our way up to the lounge areas.

On night crossings, 'Lounge Area' is a bit of a misnomer; dormitory would be a better word.

Although there were far more people behind us than in front in the queue to board, already there is barely a free inch of banquette as the first passengers up the stairs selfishly lie down, full length, shoes on, most of them, and give not a tinker's cuss for any of their fellow passengers who might like a little piece of banquette for themselves. Fortunately for us, we prefer a comfy chair with table to that of a fully prone crossing, so we find a window seat with table so I can stare out at nothing for virtually the whole journey.

We watch a constant stream of passengers searching for somewhere to sit, all looking contemptuously at those early birds who are pretending to sleep, it's impossible that they are asleep but they act the part well.

"Coffee?" She nods, but when I get up to fetch it, I notice the queue seems to stretch back to Carmarthen, so I suggest we hang on a bit.

Still people continue to arrive, many with kids; there's hardly any seating available now – the ferry company really should do something about it. Announcements are useless because of course the people they are addressing are 'asleep'.

We are on board for maybe 35-40 minutes when the Tannoy comes to life with the safety messages about where the life jackets are stored and the appropriate mustering stations for each deck. By now there isn't that much carpet visible, though I do delight in watching three guys dressed in Irish Rugby shirts suggesting to a chap lying on a banquette that he might enjoy the crossing more in a seated position!

"Are we moving?" Head Office is not the greatest of sailors, she got a bit woozy on the Isle of Wight ferry. I help with, "Unless Fishguard is going backwards," but at this hour of the morning her funny bone is asleep even if the rest of her isn't. She surely isn't turning green already?

The Tannoy cackles to life again.

"Good morning, ladies and gentlemen, this is your Captain, Edward John Smith (I made that bit up), speaking. On behalf of Colander Ferries (and that bit), I should like to welcome you to our 2.30 a.m. crossing to Rosslare. I can advise that we will be utilising the ship's stabilisers this morning, as the weather conditions, certainly for the first part of the journey, are a little windy. The wind is forecast to drop off a bit later, so hopefully the second part of the crossing will be more comfortable." I couldn't get out of my mind the thought of two small jockey wheels being extended from the sides of the ship. Stabilisers?

We hadn't been moving for any more than a minute when

the ship groaned and shook in rivet-loosening fashion. I looked at the crew members I could just see behind the lounge bar; they didn't bat an eyelid, so I thought calls to abandon ship a little premature. Head Office on the other hand looked at me with an expression which said, *WTF?* I just shrugged and watched the lights of Fishguard move ever so slowly further away.

I'm also no sailor, but I do have a stronger constitution for the sea than a lot of people. Even so, it wasn't long after leaving the somewhat sheltered harbour behind, that the first tummy testing roll and dip occurred; this was quickly followed by the next one, then a third much worse than the first two. Suddenly, everyone who was standing or returning to their seats seemed drunk. People carrying drinks were timing their steps to the flat part of the roll, desperately trying to keep whatever fluid they were carrying horizontal, adopting as wide a gait as possible in the hope that this might in some way counterbalance the moving floor.

I noticed that there were now fewer people both at the bar and in the cafeteria area, "Coffee?"

After many years of marriage, sometimes words just aren't needed, there's a symbiosis between partners that renders verbal communication an unnecessary interloper; this was one of those moments. Head Office no longer wanted a drink.

Passengers were now doing the mental arithmetic of how fast they could get to the toilets.

I didn't realise at the time, but Head Office had purposely chosen the table we were at for its proximity to the facilities. This was both a good idea and not such a good idea. Good of course because should the need arise, access would be swift, bad because the door wouldn't latch properly, or people just didn't have time, consequently it banged like a sailor on shore leave. Great thwacking thunderclaps, two or three a minute; this will be fun for nearly four hours, I thought. Of course there was absolutely no option to move.

A half hour to forty minutes in and it was definitely getting worse, I think we were at the point where, in Ulysses, James Joyce described the sea as 'scrotumtightening', and as I said, I have been blessed with a fairly solid constitution when it comes to Mal de Mer, and I've had some pretty rough channel crossings to prove it. I knew I was going to be OK, but sadly I was in a very small minority. Head Office resembled an under ripe tomato. Her neck goes red when she's stressed, but her face had turned very pasty with perhaps just a hint of lime. Time to cheer her up.

"I think they're showing *The Poseidon Adventure* in the little cinema." Nothing, not even a titter.

Another downside to our nearness to the loos was that we could hear what was going on, we could hear the barfing at least. More and more crew members appeared with buckets and mops and huge rolls of oversize blue kitchen roll. This was all too much for Head Office; she rose like one of the waves outside, and with no little haste made it to the banging door. On her return some five minutes later, she delved into the Postman's Sack she uses for a handbag and pulled out a packet of Wet Wipes. Opening two, she dropped her face into them, held the pose for a few seconds, then lifted her head, rubbing her mouth with obvious displeasure. "A lot of swapping recipes in there?" I asked.

It stayed pretty much the same for another hour or so, a

steady flow both to and inside the loos, no respecter of gender is vomitus eruptus. I chose this moment to fetch myself a coffee, there was no queue at all. I did wonder should I take back a great big greasy spoon of a breakfast, but I would probably have been cast overboard. I passed Head Office a bottle of still water.

"I think it might be easing a touch," I offered. She gave the faintest of nods, she leaned back and shut her eyes, the wet wipes still balled in her fist.

The Irish Sea was becoming less angry, no millpond, but you could walk the ship's corridors without bumping off one wall to the other and the lavvy door was banging much less.

I looked around the lounge, it was like a scene from Scutari portrayed in those old films. People lying on the floor, foetal, with rucksacks as pillows. People adopting all sorts of angles across chairs and benches, just trying to get comfy, finally enjoying the slightly gentler crossing, babies being nursed by rocking mothers and older kids asleep across dads' knees. I went for a walk.

Ferry shops, on the Irish Sea, are a great place to shop, particularly if your passion in life is anything tacky with the word Guinness blazed across it. Whole walls and stands of everything you could possibly imagine, from key rings to scarves and thimbles to umbrellas, writing sets to waterproof jackets. As far as I could see, the only thing you couldn't buy emblazoned with Guinness, was Guinness. Leprechauns and other little people in various guises came a not very close second in the Tacky Races.

I browsed my way through the T-shirts, these were mostly crested with the logo 'Ireland' written in some kind of Celtic script but were closely followed by you know what. The watches tempted me; I had decided a new watch would be my present to myself on this trip. I bought a newspaper and some cough sweets and returned to see how Head Office was faring. She was in the same head-back position, but I noticed she'd managed an inch of water. I let her be and went for another walk.

There's actually not a lot to see on these big ferries, and big they are, many at 40,000 tonnes plus and carry up to 1,500 passengers. There might be five, six, or seven car and heavy vehicle decks with usually a maximum of two passenger decks, half of which might be taken up with individual cabins, for those who don't like community barfing.

Every available space not filled by the facilities will be filled with Video Games and One-Armed Bandits. They belch, bleep, and bang at you constantly. You have to ever be on the lookout for speeding cars or being strafed by errant machine gun fire. Just making the short trip from the café back to your seat means you have to run a gauntlet of electronic farts.

The sea has become much calmer now and people are emerging from their hapless cocoons and starting to sit up straight and once more take an interest in tea and coffee. This is emphasised as I walk back to the lounge area via a now much busier cafeteria than when I last went by.

Back at our table, Head Office had a little colour back. "Fancy some fresh air?" She nodded. We put on our coats and covered our chairs with the newspaper and a magazine. There were a number of exits out on to the viewing deck and as smoking had yet to be banned, many of the people out there were doing just that. The 'snotgreen sea', Joyce again, could now be made out as dawn was breaking at our backs. The sea actually still looked pretty rough – good old stabilisers thought I, they really are working. Head Office looked ahead, desperate for her first glimpse of her beloved Ireland, straining over the rail for a little sight of land.

We went back inside, and she said she could probably manage a coffee now, so I went and joined the queue. When I returned with the coffees, it had got much lighter and she was sat where I had been, so she was looking forward, ever desperate for that first view of *home*.

Before long she drew my attention and with a big beaming smile, a thing not thought possible an hour earlier, she pointed dead ahead. I twisted in my chair and saw what I first thought was low-lying cloud but soon realised it was actually low-lying land. The crossing teases you a bit here, because you can see land, you think, almost there, when in fact you will have at least an hour, perhaps more before disembarkation.

With the advancing light and the quieter sea, the whole lounge area now stirred from its torpor; toilets, now miraculously clean, were being used for their original purpose, and the more familiar aroma of coffee percolated into the area.

"Toast?" I ask.

"No thanks," says she, so I venture that I'll just go and get a couple of slices; keep the wolf from the door etc. I return with two slices of toast and two more coffees. As I start to butter my first slice she says, "I'll just have half a slice." Inside my head I scream, *I would have bought three effing slices had you not said you didn't want any.* I smile and very lightly butter her a very small half slice.

The harbour lights are coming alongside now, and the

intercom communicates instruction to the various types of travellers. Foot passengers go here, those on buses go there, car drivers go thither. Although the instructions actually start with, "In a few minutes we will ask …", most people completely ignore the first part of the instruction and rush to take up their positions straight away. To be fair, I too stand and start to assemble our stuff together, but the seasoned traveller that Head Office is tells me to sit down as it will be at least fifteen minutes before they open the stairs to the car decks.

She is of course correct, but when the call to return to our cars does come, the stampede to get to the correct deck would not have been any more frantic had the call been to man the lifeboats.

Once back with the car, I take the dogs' water dish out, empty it on the deck, and get in. All around are signs telling drivers not to start their cars until told to do so. Cars are starting up all about me; deck personnel are now working in a fog of carbon monoxide, but already one of the lines is starting to exit. I notice the car three in front of mine start slowly to edge forward, and we too taxi our way along the car lane before emerging in the fresh light of day that is Ireland.

What we actually emerge onto is a long metallic ramp which guides us down on to terra firma. As we start to head for the port exit, the flow of traffic divides either side of a Hi-Viz tabarded policeman, though here of course his vest says Garda. Not Customs, I notice, but Police; nevertheless absolutely no one is stopped and no vehicle is searched.

I'm expecting to be asked any minute to pull over so madam can get down on her knees and kiss the ground, but this doesn't happen. Surprisingly quickly after leaving the port, the traffic thins, and we are now at the start of our adventure; this is Ireland I'm driving through. I'm finally shaking hands with Erin, and I wonder how long that rictus grin on Head Office's face is going to last, all week probably.

Our destination was Kerry; this meant that we had to travel, in its entirety, the south coast of Ireland in one day. Not a vast distance mileage-wise, maybe 175-185 miles, but without the assistance of any motorways at all, and with very few, as yet, bypasses. This was to be seen not as a disadvantage, but more what the holiday was all about. I wanted to see Ireland and what it had to offer, what better way of seeing it than by meandering through its minor roads and country lanes, following the instructions of my navigator, who had mistakenly brought along a road map written entirely in Russian. Or so it seemed!

I pulled over, I knew we didn't want to go into Wexford town. "Let me just take a look." She passed me the road atlas. "Right," I said, "what you need to look for is a left turn which says R733. It'll be just a few kilometres up this road. We can follow that to that ferry crossing we read about."

"I know," she retorts, with an indignance that is baffling.

I fetched two coffees from a garage we stopped at and picked up the road map again. "If we head to this place," I pointed at Duncannon on the map, "it shows there's a big beach and hopefully we can give the dogs a run, and its only a couple of miles from the ferry." She confirmed this was a good idea, put on her now needed sunglasses, and off we went.

Just a few miles later we entered the village of Duncannon. The cannon part was appropriate, as one end of the large beach was the small town, which itself was dominated by an impressive fort. The fort was predominantly 16th century, and in a design known as a Star fort. This gave the stronghold a commanding presence over the River Suir estuary, or Waterford Harbour as it was called on the map.

Finding somewhere to park was no problem, as it soon became evident that the beach was quite accommodating to cars. We drove past a number of vehicles to a quite empty area and let the dogs out. The Mistress of the Stool grabbed a couple of poop bags, and we went for a good leg stretch.

The beach was long and sheltered, the wind having almost gone now, the shape of a shallow horseshoe, the sea gently sighing onto it as though tired from its immense journey.

"I'm in, you coming?"

"I most definitely am not," came the expected reply. I slipped my shoes and socks off and pulled up my trouser legs as far as they could go.

"C'mon, Honey," I shouted, and our Golden Retriever followed me in.

I threw her tennis ball a good few feet out and she bounded after it. Honey was utterly oblivious to the cold that had started to glaciate my feet; she loved the water and would have stayed in all day if it were not for the onset of my first-degree frostbite. "Jeez that's cold," I say as I use the good lady to lean on while trying to replace socks on unfeeling feet; she muttered something I didn't quite catch, it might have been "Silly bugger".

Passage East is a small community on the other side of the water, to get to which, you had to take the ferry across Waterford Harbour from Ballyhack. This fifteen-minute stretch of water is not only the boundary between Counties Wexford and Waterford but also between the provinces of Leinster (Wexford) and Munster (Waterford), a line of demarcation so important in the world of Irish sport. The ferry itself never stops, a constant toing and froing from 7.00 a.m. to 9.30 p.m. every day. It holds maybe thirty cars at a push and whenever we've used it, which is often over the years, there has always been at least half a dozen cars waiting to board at either end. I wind the window down to pay the man. Honey, as always, goes completely mental at the sight of a Hi-Viz jacket. They're supposed to be colour blind, dogs, but Honey can spot a postman at the other end of our road, and yet leave everyone else quite unbarked at.

We push on westwards and at the town of Kilmacthomas we get our first glimpse of some proper Irish scenery, the Comeragh Mountains. Not a great range in number, only twelve peaks, but, with a highest point of 2598ft, not insignificant. But it's not the height that makes the Comeragh so impressive, it's the elegance. They stand sentinel over Dungarvan bay, and like many great Irish peaks they rise at the coast, almost out of the sea, displaying their full height and majesty.

As we approach Youghal, pronounced Yawl, the road again clings to the coast or the wide Blackwater River estuary, and I notice up ahead a layby café. I didn't realise at the time, as there are so many of these in the UK, but in Ireland they are almost unheard of, because in Ireland, it's the petrol stations that have taken on the mantle of refreshing the weary traveller. I pull in.

"Coffee?"

"Yes please," she says.

"Can you manage anything to eat yet? How's the tummy doing?"

A large exhalation of breath follows; "'spose I should try."

The site has a number of picnic tables along its length and putting the leads on the dogs we move to the furthest one.

In the café I notice a trucker, his lorry the only other vehicle in the car park, pushing a knife through a delectable looking Bacon, Egg and Sausage Bap, so I order two of those; oh and an egg sandwich for H\O.

It's a beautiful morning, the still lowish sun turning the water into a giant mirror; various seabirds busy themselves along the shoreline. Head Office, perhaps it's time you knew she was called Angie, looked out over the bay.

"You OK?" I enquired; she smiled, "I'm always OK when I'm in Ireland." She threw the salivating dogs a bit of crust each, funny how they always congregate at her feet and not mine when there's food about.

I stare out at the shining sea. "It is lovely," I say.

"Gorgeous," she replies, "and you ain't seen nothing yet."

The town of Youghal was something of a bottleneck (since bypassed) but has some interesting and old buildings. One of the more surprising facts about Youghal is that Sir Walter Raleigh was once its mayor and lived there for many years. At his home, Myrtle Grove, he planted the first taters in Ireland, having brought them back from Virginia in 1585, what a part they were going to play in the history of this island!

Cork City was extremely difficult to navigate, road works and diversions everywhere. I was convinced we were going the wrong way on a number of occasions, only to spot a helpful sign, and then lose the direction again. We passed a very pretty building somewhere in the city, unfortunately it was for about the third time, when Angie had the brainwave, "Follow that car; it's got Kerry plates. Let's hope it's going home." It was a long shot of course, the bloody car might have been going to Rosslare, but it wasn't. We soon had signposts to places we knew we wanted, Macroom, Killarney; we were on our way again.

West Cork is beautiful; and when you arrive there, it all becomes so much more Irish.

I think it's the rurality that you notice. Settlements become fewer and smaller, distances between, a little longer. We were travelling the N22 towards Macroom when I suddenly realised we weren't going through town after town, village after village, sure there were some, just not as many.

Fields seemed greener in some way, and bigger, with more cows. Farmhouses a little more remote, more bucolic. The landscape had changed; hills were always the horizon. There was less traffic.

Macroom looked an attractive town with a pleasant market square area and lots of parking; so we did. We had a walk around; it was a bustling place with lots of individual and distinct small shops. Ireland is still mostly free of chain-store mania which so blights many UK high streets.

Something then happened in Macroom, on the first day of our holiday, which is absolutely true; I say this because as well as being hard to believe, it's Irish!

As mentioned previously, I intended to treat myself on this holiday to a new watch, so, naturally, when passing a jewellers, I stopped to look at the fare on offer. On display was a watch I was really taken by. I pointed it out to Ange who laughed and said, "Have you seen the price?" A sign sellotaped to the window said 'All Watches Reduced', I looked again at the watch which interested me to see that my watch had indeed been reduced to £100 from £99. My first visit to Ireland, you couldn't make it up, but there it was. A £99 sign clearly crossed through with £100 written neatly underneath.

"I do like it," I said. "Let's go in." Behind the counter was a very neatly dressed man, a walking advert for his wares, with a shiny gold matching cufflink and tie pin set and a large faced, most expensive looking watch. "I'm interested in a watch in the window," I said, "but only at the old price, not at the reduced one." He looked at me as though he hadn't heard me, moved from behind the counter, asked me which window the particular watch was displayed in and undid a sliding lock mechanism that held the wooden back panel to the display in place.

He fetched out the tray of watches mine was on and brought it back to the counter.

"Now sir?" he asked, still a little perplexed by my original question. "That's the one," I pointed. He took out the gold-faced watch with the light brown strap.

"A very nice watch, sir, would you like to try the strap for size?"

"Yes," I said, "but would you just confirm the price for me." He looked at the price ticket, hanging by fine string from the strap buckle. A slow, very engaging smile started to spread across his face and ended in a small chuckle.

"Sir you can most certainly have this watch for the original price of £99 if you wish, or you can have it at the now further reduced and correct price of £89, should you so desire." He carried on, "I can't even blame anyone else – it's my handwriting. I need a holiday, sir," he sighed with a smile. "Well I'm having one," I said, "and buying the watch will give it a perfect start. I'll take it." We left the shop with a cordial thank you from behind the counter and continued our stroll up the street. As the shops ran out, we crossed over and retraced our steps back along the opposite pavement, where we noticed the jeweller standing outside his shop studiously examining the prices on display in his sale.

We liked Macroom. Its Castle and Town Hall dominated the town but not in an overpowering way. For such prominent buildings there is a definite subtlety to their grandeur. There is also a very splendid 10 arch bridge over the River Sullane.

It was just south of Macroom, at *Beal na Blath* that the revolutionary soldier and politician, Michael Collins, was killed in an ambush in 1922, more of which later.

We continued our journey west on the N22 heading in the direction of Killarney.

Soon the horizon was broken by the Derrynasaggart Mountains; again, not a great range but imposing enough, rising to over 2,200 ft. From now on, our time in Kerry and Cork would almost always be dominated by one range of hills or another.

We pushed on, the expedition navigator slowly becoming more confident. "We're looking for a right turn just up here," she advised.

"Right?" I asked, she manoeuvred the road map through

180 degrees.

"No, left," she said, adding, "you knew what I meant!" We reached a junction signed R569 Kenmare. "This is us," she imperiously announced.

"We need to find somewhere for the dogs, we don't want them jumping out of the car and crapping all over somebody's lawn the second we get there." No sooner had I said this, when Angie pointed out to the right, a rough track leading into an area of woodland. I pulled over. As the dogs sniffed, cocked, squatted, and evacuated, we took in the woodland and surrounding views. "It's beautiful," I said, the sun casting long shadows across the car. Herself just beamed.

Like weary desert travellers with an Oasis in sight, we started the last two or three miles into Kilgarvan with renewed gusto.

We were renting a cottage, and though the address was nominally Kilgarvan, our instructions were to head for a Motor Museum. As we drove into Kilgarvan, we were met with the now familiar houses and buildings decorated in various pastel shades, blues, greens, greys, and it seemed a preponderance of light terracotta. A tight main street snaked its way through the town, giving residence to a number of small shops, cafés, and pubs, that at first sight seemed to be owned by the same family. We saw no semblance of anything that looked like a Motor Museum, and were contemplating turning round and having another look, when, just after the Healy Rae Petrol Station and Convenience Store, we noticed a brown sign on the left. Sure enough, it said Motor Museum, 2km.

In Ireland, at the time of our first visit, before there was any Motorway network to speak of, (apart from the M1 and one small section of the M7, the rest were on the drawing board) roads were classified as N, R, or L, still are actually. I have always assumed that this stood for National, Regional, and Local, I may be way off the mark with that but it's as good a description as I can think of. The road we were now travelling on fell most definitely into the L category. Not quite grass growing up the middle of the road, though there are still plenty of those, but very twisty and in many places difficult for two vehicles to pass without extreme caution. Another sign, this time hand-painted, confirmed we were still going in the right direction. Above this sign a more intriguing one. Another conventional brown information sign indicated that we were also going in the direction of Macaura's Grave. We continued to climb, leaving a very fast-flowing stream down wooded banks to our left. The road suddenly widened slightly, and a single lamppost indicated a driveway leading up to the right. The lamppost was standing over a large boulder on which was written Motor Museum, with a white painted arrow underneath. We drove up the gravelled drive, coming to stop in front of a pretty house, that had large areas of hard standing, well trimmed hedges, and many shrubs.

We got out and I rang the doorbell, as Angie was trying to shush the dogs who, having been quiet for most of the journey, now decided it was time to go embarrassingly mental.

A friendly and engaging lady came to the door. "Hello there," I said, "Andrew and Angela Knowles, we've come for the cottage." She introduced herself, and completely ignoring the dogs, indicated we should follow her, at the same time making friendly small talk, commenting on the fine weather and asking if we had had a good trip. The cottage was a small annexe to the side of her own house. She opened the front door and handed me a set of keys. She quickly showed us round, telling us where the fundamentals were, and saying she was only next door if there was anything at all we needed, or she could help us with. Just before she left, she went to the small, pine dining table in the kitchen area and lifted a tea towel off a plate of six delicious looking scones. "I made these this morning," she said, "thought you might be a bit peckish." We thanked her wholeheartedly and with that she left us.

We let her get back to her own house before we ventured out for the dogs and cases. Having unloaded, I left Angie to do the jobs I only get in the way of and ventured outside for another look round. We had climbed quite a way from the village, and I knew that in front of us would be a splendid view but for the high thick trees that surrounded the property. Into my head popped that old Music Hall monologue:

Wiv a ladder an some glarses
You could see the 'Ackney Marshes
If it wasn't for the 'ouses in between.

Further along to the left of our cottage were two large barns. A door to the first was ajar so I popped my head through, there was no one about so I ventured in. This was the Motor Museum, or at least part of it.

This was petrol head heaven and though I could accurately be described as not one of those, I do love history and old things and it was clear that these rooms were full of both. This wasn't Beaulieu, in fact the less than immaculate show on offer was very refreshing. It was like being in a mad scientist's garage; shelves of old parts and tools, stacks of tyres of all sorts and sizes, many just leaning against each other in any spare area that could be filled.

It must have been a real labour of love to get all those vehicles, in various states of disrepair, up that track and into situ, and I'd only seen a half of it!

I ventured back to the cottage. Angie was putting away a few essentials we'd brought with us, Dog Food, Dog Biscuits, Dog Treats. She turned and said, "That nice lady has left us fresh milk, a small loaf, tea, coffee and sugar, isn't that thoughtful?"

"It is, has she left us any beer or wine?" I interpreted the glare as a No. "We'd better go shopping then."

We left the dog's big cushions on the floor and chucked a throw we carry over the settee, just in case they didn't want to slum it any more, then set off back down into the village.

The Healy Rae convenience store provided just enough provender and alcohol for the evening, so we bought what we needed, and decided we would have to find a bigger store tomorrow, even though it would be Sunday. We decided to check out Kenmare, about 10 minutes away.

As you arrive into Kenmare you are welcomed on your left by the lusciously green and finely manicured fairways, greens, and bunkers of the Kenmare Golf Club, an establishment which immediately struck one as not being inexpensive! Whether it is or not, I never got the chance to find out. I am someone who does like to bat a ball about a bit, but the good lady doesn't, so when it came to loading the car, and it was Clubs or Dogs, you know who won!

Kenmare immediately strikes one as a bit touristy. Not in an over tackily way: it's just that there are a few more gift shops than are usually found. There are, however, a lot more pubs, eating establishments, and hotels, which would generally suggest a town with a high visitor frequency. This is not really surprising as it is a gateway town: first and foremost to the fabulous Ring of Kerry, to be explored later, but also the lesser celebrated, but equally impressive, Beara Peninsula. Coupled with these it gives dramatic mountainous access to Glengarriff, Bantry, and the Sheepshead Peninsula.

The main thoroughfares of Kenmare are a triangle of roads. The base of this isocelesian cuteness is the continuation of the road you travel in on. Once over a small roundabout, the shortest or top of the three roads that form a triangle, contains a few retail outlets, a couple of bars, a hotel, and a number of B&Bs.

At the next mini roundabout, a right turn brings you on to a very busy, colourful, and bustling street of shops, bars, and cafes. To the left at the bottom of this road were more shops and hostelries which were just across from a well-appointed park area.

To the right was the third leg of our triangle, another plethora of pubs, cafes, and gift shops with the odd bank and grocery store thrown in.

A nice town, busy with pavement clogging, window-watching tourists, that gave it a vibrant well-to-do ambience. I liked it.

Driving back to Kilgarvan, we both said how we were looking forward to further exploring Kenmare in the coming week.

"Fancy a pint?"

"Why not," she replies, pulling the passenger visor down, and, delving into her handbag, pulls out a hairbrush.

There was of course an Elephant in the car!

We had made a mistake, a mistake that we would never make again in all our subsequent visits: we had chosen a cottage an unsuitably long way from the nearest pub.

"I'll drive tonight," I said, with just the faintest, almost undetectable emphasis on the 'tonight'.

I pulled up just past the Jackie Healy Rae Bar. On the pavement by the corner of the pub were, neatly stacked, fifteen or sixteen empty beer barrels. Above the door, the inevitable, if not obligatory, Guinness sign.

"Guinness please," I asked of the pleasant face behind the bar, "and a," I turned, 'Pint' was mouthed back at me, "Pint of lager please."

"No problem, take a seat I'll bring 'em over to ya."

Bring them over to me? This was different. I did as I was asked and joined Ange who was already seated. Almost immediately, or so it seemed, the barman reappeared with a pint of lager, which he placed on the beer mat he carried with him, on the table in front of Ange. The barman retraced his steps, I assumed to fetch my Guinness, but no, he walked to the end of the bar where he continued chatting to the bloke he was talking with when we walked in.

I gave it a moment or two and looked at Ange. "He's forgotten mine," I whispered.

"Don't be silly," she replied with a knowing smile. "It'll be on its way." I looked again at the inactivity behind the bar.

I whispered again, "We're only here for a week." She teasingly drained a half inch of lager, endorsing the pleasure with a satisfied sigh.

"Nice?" I asked, in a somewhat pointed manner. What seemed like hours later, but was probably no more than a minute, I noticed her nod towards the bar. The barman was finishing pouring a pint of Guinness. He was clearly taking great care over the procedure. As he returned the pump handle to the vertical, he picked up another beer mat and proceeded to deliver me my first pint of 'Irish' Guinness. As he placed it in front of me, he said "Enjoy" and as I scrambled to get my wallet out to pay him, he raised a hand and said, "No rush, no rush," and returned to his bar duties.

What sat in front of me looked decidedly perfect, a Zurbaran still life could not have captured its exquisiteness better.

I looked at Ange. "So let's run over what just happened here, we've walked into a bar we've never been in before; we've been met with a friendly face; I've ordered two drinks which arrived by waiter service; the barman has told me there's no rush to pay, and the beer is …" I picked up my glass and took a couple of healthy swallows, "magnificent. Just like home," I said. "Not."

Ange leaned into me, smiled, and said, "I told you you'd like it here."

We finished our drinks, I paid the barman, he gave me my change, thanked me, and invited me to "Come again". I told him we most definitely would.

Back at the cottage, the very long day was catching up with me. I sat at a bench just outside the lounge window, poured myself a large glass of Merlot, and watched as the dogs busied themselves with all the smells of those dogs that had passed before. Ange was cooking, and singing, *(sic)* and all was most definitely well with the world.

CHAPTER 2

Sunday

SLEEP UNTIL YOU'RE HUNGRY THEN EAT UNTIL YOU'RE SLEEPY

I was woken in the early hours of Sunday morning by one of three things, though it's more likely to have been a combination of all three.

Firstly, there was a biblical thunderstorm going on outside. I could hear the trees fighting against being uprooted and the rain belting into the corrugated roof of the nearby museum. The wind was tempestuous, and howled like a fabled local Banshee, and the chains that the Museum sign hung from, creaked like the ghost of Christmas Past.

As if this wasn't bad enough, our Golden Retriever, who was the second worse snorer in the world, had somehow inveigled herself on to the bottom of the bed and was really letting rip.

To cap all of this, the world's worst, or should that be best, or loudest, snorer was lying at the side of me.

I was trapped, pinned down by the deadweight of big dog lying on the duvet, and so had real trouble in extricating myself from the bed. I finally managed to contort myself into a position of freedom; a couple of grunts came from the bed, though from which blonde they emanated I couldn't be certain.

I stood at the window, fascinated by the wildness of the dancing trees and the low cloud rushing across the sky, allowing fleeting glimpses of a three-quarter moon. A plastic plant pot skipped and jumped across the hard standing, coming to rest against the museum wall.

I walked through to the kitchen, made a cup of tea, and returned to the bedroom. I put on my bedside lamp and grabbed Honey by the collar. "Sorry old girl," I muttered, as she plaintively looked up at me, "but it's you or her." I read for as long as it took to drink my tea and then dropped off again.

A few hours later I was awake once more, this time with the sun streaming through curtains that didn't quite meet in the middle. The half inch or so gap conceding a pencil-thin streak of light across the room.

I took Sleeping Beauty a coffee and gathered up the dogs.

There were woods all around us and though there were no clearly defined paths, there was also an absence of 'Keep Out' signs. So, walking boots donned, we set out to explore. The morning could not have been more different than the storms of the night. The last vestiges of what was quite a wind, now gently swayed the upper branches, marbling the forest floor with flecks of light. The air was thin and fresh and filled the nostrils with the musk of a thousand years of rotting vegetation. We didn't venture too far; the trees were dense and it would have been easy to lose one's bearings once any of the Museum buildings were out of sight. I wasn't really worried; I had my canine compass. If I did happen to become disorientated, I would have simply looked Honey in the eye and asked "Where's Angie?" and she, as sure as eggs is eggs, would have led me straight back. After a few more minutes of playing Grizzly Adams and having ensured the dogs had 'made void', we retraced our path.

Over a slice or two of toast we determined our plan for the day. Angie did not enjoy driving, and we had already decided that I would do it all (apart from the odd trip back from the pub) whilst in Ireland. This suited me, as I don't very much enjoy being a passenger, so, after the long day at the wheel yesterday, we decided not to venture too far today. We also both fancied another look at Kenmare.

We aimed for Killarney. The road map suggested a nice circular route so we started by retracing our steps to Kenmare; we wouldn't stop there this morning but would revisit for a good look round this afternoon.

Soon, tantalising brown signs promise Moll's Gap and Lakes View. The road starts to climb, now just rough pasture on either side of the road, the horizon becoming corrugated with the outline of hills. Suddenly there are generous, breathtaking views to the east, down glacial valleys, peppered with sheep. Every few hundred yards or so, there are small areas where the road has been widened and small lay-bys appear. Almost all contain an empty car with three or four people stood to the side taking photographs. As we climb higher, peaks on either side of the road suggest we are nearing Molls Gap.

The Gap itself is the highest point on this part of the Ring. It is named after one Moll Kissane who, with an eye to the main chance, in the 1820s set up a *Sibin,* effectively an unlicensed drinking house for the men who were building the road; whether or not it offered any other services is unrecorded. It affords wonderful views to the distant Macgillycuddy's Reeks, a most dramatic range of mountains that incorporate a number of 3,000ft peaks, including Ireland's highest mountain, Carrauntoohill which stands at 3,406ft, though is often difficult to pinpoint exactly.

We pull into the ample car park; the ubiquitous café and gift shop awaits.

Suitably refreshed, we continue, now downhill all the way, with even more stunning views. Directly in front of us and to our right there are now large plantations of pine, giving the road an almost alpine feel. To our left, a deep valley floor, puddled with small lakes and interlocking streams.

Further on still, we come to another area of off-road parking and buildings. This is Ladies' View, a dazzling, panoramic vista framed into a V shape by the mountain slopes either side. A river valley and more lakes, olive and pea green fields of pasture, run through with a silvery sapphire blade of water. How lucky we were to see it at its most exquisite, on such a beautiful, cloudless morning. Old 'Head Office' has banged on about how beautiful Kerry is for the last ten years and though this is only my first full day here, I cannot fault her judgement.

Entering Killarney on the Ring Road you are immediately struck by the number and quality of the hotels on offer. This is the Muckross area of town and is clearly the neighbourhood you would look for work if you were a burglar. We pass a couple of signs for Muckross Abbey, House and Gardens and give a nod to each other that we would visit later in the week. There are also signs for Jaunting Cars, though as yet I have no idea what these are. It seems there is a billboard for almost every hotel in town, suddenly we are on a bridge over a wide river which affords magnificent views over the distant Reeks and you suddenly begin to realise just why this might be.

The centre of Killarney is arrived at via a large tree-filled roundabout and at this point resembles more the Wild West than the West of Ireland. A large off-road lay-by is filled with 10 or more horse-driven stagecoaches; these are a tad smaller than the John Wayne version and are obviously the famed Jaunting Cars. They are covered four-wheel wagons, which would comfortably (?) take four or six passengers, but I'm disappointed that none of the drivers are wearing cowboy hats or boots. We drive on into the town centre and up the high street, a busy, colourful, bustling area; jam packed with shops, cafés, and pubs. We pass a striking church which turns out to be the impressive St Mary's Cathedral. We continue on, through and around the town for a few more minutes.

We both like what we see and agree that we will save Killarney for the end of the week or the first bad day we get, weather-wise.

We spot an All Routes signpost and follow this until we meet the N22 Macroom, Cork road. We follow this until we arrive at the same junction we turned off at yesterday, the R569 which will bring us to Kilgarvan.

After a leisurely late lunch, Angie walked the dogs into the woods while I chilled with the day's paper.

"Fancy Kenmare then?" I asked, as she strolled back into view, the dogs having beaten her back.

"Yeah, let's," she said.

"Great," I replied. "I'll drive there."

Re-tracing our route of yesterday, we set off back down the hill to Kilgarvan then left to Kenmare. Just as we arrived at the outskirts of Kenmare, we both burst out laughing. I came to an abrupt halt, checked the mirror, and started reversing some forty yards back up the road, both of us still chuckling, Angie saying she'd never seen anything like it, and I most certainly hadn't. I pulled into the side of the road as best I could and switched on the hazards. I wound Angie's window down so we could get a better look.

There, on the grass verge between pavement and road, tethered to a small tree, happily munching away, was a white horse. This horse was like none I had ever seen before, because all along its flank, in green paint of some description, was written, UP KERRY. I had noticed both yesterday and this morning the abundance of green and gold flags or pennants, hung from every vantage point available. Bunting hung from or between houses or lampposts or houses and telegraph poles or lampposts and telegraph poles. Larger flags adorned almost every garden or gatepost. No road sign was left unflagged. It now dawned on me that we were back in GAA territory, and the flags and bunting were a show of support for 'The Kingdom', as the Kerry team were known.

"They must have a game today," I said to Ange as we continued on into Kenmare, now even more aware of the decoration. In fact, houses without some form or other of the green and gold on display were few and far between.

We parked up near the church and walked back towards the main drag. A few yards in we came to an Irish theme park in the guise of one of the biggest gift shops I've ever been in. There cannot be anything in the entire history of the Irish

Gift industry that was not on sale in this shop.

It was fabulous. Downstairs was all that you would expect to find from such an emporium. Just think of anything you can stick the word Ireland on, and they had it. A lot of it was, surprisingly, quite exquisite, and we ummed and aahhed over a few items. Upstairs there was an even greater opportunity to spend a lot of money. Coats, jackets, suits, jumpers, shoes, luxurious scarves, real top-notch stuff.

Angie was gently fondling and clearly taken with a scarf.

"Go on," I said, "have it."

"Have you seen how much it is?" she retorted.

"Is it more or less than my watch?" I asked.

"That's not the point," she said, putting it back and moving to look at some shoes.

She has always been personally parsimonious my wife, trying to get her to spend money on herself was like getting blood from a stone. If I wanted anything, like the watch yesterday, no problem. I inwardly vowed to get us back in the shop before the end of the week; she will have her scarf.

On this occasion, however, we managed to escape with our entire fortune still intact.

I fancied a pint; the pretty pub next door was rammed with people eating, so we moved to a larger pub over the road. This pub was also packed, and with a television on almost every wall it was pretty obvious why. Angie spotted two seats at a bench just round the corner from the door, probably only free because you had to crane your neck to see a telly. I fought my way through to the bar.

Now, the Irish have a reputation for enjoying the odd pint,

not an unjust or unfair observation the subsequent years have taught me, but what greeted me at the bar astonished me. The entire work surface at the back of the bar, the area under the optics where you might find ice buckets or cordial bottles or any of the other necessary bar paraphernalia, was completely covered in three-quarter filled pint glasses of Guinness. This was a big, long bar. There must have been, it's easy to exaggerate, but over a hundred glasses, or near as damn it. Customers at the bar, and many behind, were ordering in semaphore. A hand would go up with five fingers extended, or perhaps four. Two hands might go up indicating six or seven or whatever number was required. When spotted one of the numerous barmen would grab a tray and finish off the requisite number of pints. At the far end of the bar two younger staff members were three-quarter filling the replacements.

A barman caught my eye. "A Guinness if you have one," I asked, smiling at my own little joke, the barman smiled as well. "And a half of Lager please." I felt I ought to have whispered the last bit. Looking round I could see two things this pub was shy of: lager drinkers were certainly one and, as far as I could tell, Angie was about female number three in a cast of thousands.

I manoeuvred the drinks back to our table, where Angie was chatting to an older guy sat to her right. "Well," I said, pointing at one of the TVs, "this explains the flags." I leaned over at the old guy who acknowledged me with a slight nod. "Who are they playing?" I asked, I had in a Holmesian manner deduced that one of the teams was Kerry, the colour of one sides shirts matched the three million flags we'd driven past on the way in.

"They're playing Kildare," he obliged, and carried on, "It's the semi-final of Sam." Noticing my perplexed face he leaned further into us, "The Sam Maguire, it's the All Ireland trophy for the football." He smiled and went on, "He was a Cock man was Sam, but we'll forgive him that: sure, we can't all be born in Kerry." He gently smiled at his own little put down.

Cock, I understood to be the local dialect for Cork.

"How are we doing?" I asked, immediately allying myself to the green and gold.

"OK," he replied, but with a slight frowning shake of the head. "Kildare is a good team this year," he leaned in again. "We won it last year but this year ..." he slightly frowned again and did not complete the sentence.

I looked at Angie who had died and gone to heaven ... again! She was sitting in a pub in Kerry listening to a nice old guy who sounded just like her late father. A loud cheer went up, Kerry had another point. It broke Angie's reverie. I said, "This is only the semi, can you imagine what it's like in here if they make the final," then added "and win it?"

A few minutes later I made my way back to the bar, it took me two or three minutes to get anyone's attention, so I usefully used the time to see if I could get my head around this game that everyone was so engrossed in. To an Englishman brought up on Cricket, Football, and Rugby, I was struggling to find the allure in what was before me. You could obviously kick it, it was called football after all (though not as we know it, Jim), but you could pass it by hand, punch it, slap it. I hadn't seen anybody head it yet but no doubt you could. The target area to score was a combination of Rugby posts and a conventional goal; imagine a Rugby pitch with the area below the bar netted up like a Football goal. One point was scored if your team propelled the ball over the bar *a la* Rugby and three points were scored if you got the ball into the goal *a la* Football.

"Two pints of Guinness and a glass of lager please." A young lady serving me this time. I paid and turned to return to our table, only just in the nick of time, the half time whistle went, and I nearly got crushed in the stampede!

I passed our newfound friend a pint, "Cheers," I said. "All the best."

"That's very kind of you indeed, many thanks," he replied.

"Andrew, this is Pat," said Angie with a beaming smile, I wanted to reply, 'Of course it bloody is', but didn't, I simply lifted my glass and said again, "All the best, Pat."

He lifted his glass by return and continued leaning in towards Angie and was no doubt being regaled with where her dad was born, and when, when he came to England and what he did. "Mum's from Ballinamore in Co. Letrim," I heard.

I stood up to get my bearings for a visit to the loo. Swirls of cigarette smoke filled the room as though the half time-whistle was also a starting gun for lighting up. I made my way across the room, weaving like a nifty fly-half, in and out of patrons going to or returning from the bar. A door at the far end led to a short passageway whose walls were wallpapered with pictures of Kerry teams, past and present, both Football and Hurling. Hurling I hadn't seen much of, but from the brief glances I had, could safely be described as a game for mad people!

I made my way back to our seats, the bar crowd now more settled as the game was about to restart.

"What do you reckon then, Pat?" I nodded in the direction of the nearest screen. "Will they do it?"

"I don't know," he said, unsure. "They're a point down at half time and they've had the wind first half," I didn't laugh, it clearly wasn't meant in jest.

Angie and I continued to sit there soaking in the atmosphere, the Oohs the Aahs the "Shoots" getting progressively louder and more animated as the match went on and the beer went down. It was clearly a very close game; even Pat let go the odd expletive. In the end, Kerry's efforts were just thwarted by Kildare and they lost by one point, 0-13 to 1-9 so though Kerry scored the only goal of the game, the aggregate score was 13-12 to Kildare.

Pat stood up and in his gentle Kerry burr said, "'Tis the way, now what'll you have?" Ange declined with, "I'm driving, Pat, thanks." I just nodded my concordance.

"'Tis the way," I said to Ange, when Pat had moved out of earshot.

"He's lovely isn't he," she replied.

"Ah, to be sure you'd think Ned Kelly was a fine man just because he's Oirish," I replied in possibly the worst vocal caricature ever attempted. She shook her head in a much better, 'we are not amused', impersonation. "Ah, go on, go on, go on go on," I retorted, this time winning a semblance of a smile.

The pub had thinned a little now the match was over, the atmosphere both a little less tumultuous and a lot less smoky. General chatter had taken over from the now silent television sets, and in the far corner I could see a young girl seeming to tune a violin. "I think there's going to be music soon," I said to

Ange and pointed out the young girl. No sooner had I done this than a man walked into the pub carrying a guitar case.

Pat returned with the drinks, put mine down in front of me, then squeezed back onto his bench seat. He sat with an exaggerated sigh and puff of the cheeks. "Are you tired, Pat?" I asked. "The match worn you out," I said, nodding at the now blank screen.

"Just not getting any younger," he replied and, picking up his glass, looked to Ange then me and said "Slainte" which is a beautiful word the way the Irish pronounce it. I responded with "Cheers. All the best." We stayed and chatted for another half hour or so. To be fair it was mostly Ange that chatted. He was a nice old boy was Pat, he had a most infectious laugh, and a very kindly smile. Angie had certainly taken to him. I was left thinking that this was the first Irishman I'd ever had a chat with, in Ireland, and if they were all like this, that'd do for me.

CHAPTER 3

Monday

MAY YOUR COFFEE BE STRONG AND YOUR MONDAY BE SHORT!

Peter Kay does a wonderful piece in his stage show about misheard lyrics and now I confess to mine. I always thought that the first line of that old classic Irish song, 'Whiskey in the Jar', was "As I was going over the Cork and Kerry mountains", but now my bubble has been well and truly pricked, I'm astonished to read that it actually is:

As I was going over the far famed Kerry mountains.

(At least that's what the Lyric website I'm looking at says.)

I like mine/Thin Lizzy's better, but that aside, if there were such a designated area as the Cork and Kerry mountains, then today we are going over them. The N71 south out of Kenmare takes you over the border into Cork.

Even more dramatic than yesterday's ride into Killarney, this serpentine road climbs and climbs and has had to be hewn from the rock in many sections: a scarred granite wall, inches from the car on one side, and blistering views dropping away on the other. In a number of places small tunnels have had to be excavated, making an aperture in the rock face, allowing an extremely tight, breathe in, passage.

Again, the vistas are extraordinary, and we have been blessed with another beautiful day. We descend into a heavily wooded valley that's taking us to our next stop, Glengarriff. Before we get to the village, we take a short climb up through the woods, this brings us to a stunning viewpoint over Glengarriff itself and, plopped into Bantry Bay just offshore, the small island which is one of our destinations for the day, Garinish (or Garnish – English?) Island. In the distance, the much larger island of Whiddy can be seen. In January 1979, an oil tanker called Betelgeuse exploded at the oil terminal situated at the far end of this island, resulting in the loss of fifty lives and dreadful ecological contamination of the surrounding coast and shoreline. We retrace our steps back down the hillside and head for the village.

The small ferry from Glengarriff to Garnish runs every thirty minutes. You see dozens of basking seals almost immediately; the island shore and small rocky outcrops are teeming with them. They are of great interest to Honey and Jess, who can't take their eyes off them as we sail close by.

About halfway across, the ticket collector/guide points out to us a charming looking house on the far side of the narrow inlet.

"Have yous heard of the fillum star, Maureen O'Hara; you know, she made fillums with John Wayne, *The Quiet Man*?" he paused just a moment, "and some cowboy fillums and the like." He continued, "Well, that house there, the white one, is where Miss O'Hara still lives to this day. She is Glengarriff's most faaaamous resident." He was unquestionably proud of this fact; you could tell from the tenor and tone of his voice that just being able to relate such an actuality gave him immense joy. Some of the other trippers asked him a few questions about her. He was clearly in his element as he told them she was nearly eighty and, no she wasn't seen about Glengarriff a lot, just occasionally, though he himself had seen her many times of course.

As the small boat reached the slipway onto the island, a few more of the preening, moustachioed seals slipped gracefully into the water, and we stepped ashore.

At the ticket office, in exchange for our fare we were given a small gatefold information brochure telling us about Garnish. One of the first things I noticed was that the gardens were designed by Harold Peto, not a household name but, close to where we lived in Wiltshire, we had come across, down a back road between Warminster and Bath, a two-arch bridge over the River Frome. The centre piece of this was a life-sized statue of some naked Roman or Greek warrior. It really took one by surprise when first encountered. Over this bridge was the splendid country pile of Iford Manor, which I had subsequently learned was the home of Harold Peto. So here was an odd connection between where we lived and where we were visiting that was completely unknown prior to our visit.

The gardens and overall design of Garinish are very impressive and, it being late August, we were still seeing them at their near best. The proximity of the Gulf Stream and the sheltered geography of the island enable it to produce many exotic blooms that would struggle to flower elsewhere. Much is made of the fact that the gardens are modelled in the Italian style, similar to those at Iford Manor. There are a number of small arbors and viewing points all about the gardens, each giving breathtaking views across the bay or up to the wooded slopes of the Caha Mountains.

The island also has its own Martello Tower dating from 1805. A very sturdy structure indeed, and I'm quite sure able to keep Boney at bay, for a short while at least.

Later in the week I picked up a guide to West Cork: places to see, things to do, it mentioned Garnish Island and the Martello Tower which had in brackets after it 'Now unused', which seemed a tad superfluous to me.

We sat on one of the many garden seats that were carefully situated to give stunning views of either garden or vista. The dogs settled and we did what you are supposed to do on holiday, we relaxed.

"And chill!" I said, stretching my long legs out in front of me; the sun still had considerable warmth to it, as evidenced by Angie's head back, sunglassed face to the rays, pose. "What a gorgeous place," I said, giving Jess a scratch behind the ear. "Shall we buy it?" I asked.

"But there's no pub," she replied all too hastily.

That's my girl!

We had another amble around, slowly making our way back to the Ferry. Ferry sounds very grand for what was not much more than a dinghy with a roof. Our friendly guide welcomed us back on board, hoping we had enjoyed ourselves, and that we weren't too shattered from all the walking.

Further testimony to the unique climate enjoyed by Glengarriff and this area of West Cork is the fact that they have a Bamboo Park, which we visited next. Apart from acres of luscious bamboo, there were many other exotic plants like palms and tree ferns. The walks were well designed and maintained and, like Garnish Island, allowed stunning views over the harbour and indeed back to Garnish.

We enjoyed a cuppa and a bun and while I was waiting to be served, bought Angela one of those little panda dolls that you sit on top of your pencil. She was really moved.

Glengarriff itself was a pleasant little village, and though we didn't know it then, would be the base for our next holiday to Ireland.

Glengarriff, in a similar way to Kenmare and the Ring of Kerry, finds itself at the south-eastern end of the Ring of Beara. This is another impressive peninsula which has as a spine, the Caha Mountains. The map clearly showed that the peninsula could be dissected by a road right through the mountains, crossing the highest point at the Healy Pass, the apex of which was also the Kerry-Cork border.

We set off in a south-westerly direction along the southern edge of the Beara. The road affords lovely windows across Bantry Bay to the Sheep's Head peninsula. Soon you arrive at the small village of Adrigole, which is overlooked by the dominating Hungry Hill, the highest peak of the Caha Mountains at 2,247ft. Hungry Hill was used by Daphne Du Maurier as the title of her 1943 novel.

The road climbs quickly, and steeply, and would be utterly unnavigable without the use of numerous hairpin bends hewn from the Old Red Sandstone. Why there is a road here at all stretches the imagination. Fierce jagged rocks line the all too narrow tarmac on one side, with a deep sweeping valley on the other. Originally called the Kerry Pass, the road was eventually re-named after the well known local (Bantry) politician Tim Healy, who became the first Governor General of the Irish Free State.

A plaque at the apex of the pass gives insight into its origin.

Conceived as a 'Famine Road', the idea was to improve Ireland's infrastructure at the same time as giving employment to local men, at the height of the monstrous famine that had engulfed much of the country. There were difficulties aplenty: lack of funding, much of it thought to be siphoned off by local landowners; lack of tools, men had to make do with whatever they had, bare hands in many cases; and most crucially, lack of food. Very little sustenance might be acquired for the three and a half pence a day the men were paid. That it was built at all pays enormous credit to the skill, craft, and sheer-bloody-mindedness of the local Cork and Kerry men.

One suspects that those workers didn't have much time or inclination to take in the ravishing views that we now enjoy. Behind us, the grey snake up which we had travelled, in front of us the beautiful blue of Glanmore Lake, and in the distance the Kerry Ring.

A gentler drop down onto the Kerry side, though the landscape remains rough and rugged, flashes of the now azure Kenmare River tantalize in the distance, and eventually we arrive at the village of Lauragh, and back onto the designated ring road for the Beara Peninsula.

We can turn right here and follow the water's edge back the few miles into Kenmare, or we can turn left and complete a circumnavigation. Angie quite sensibly says, "Left, we might not get another day this nice." She is of course absolutely right.

We head west, the road sometimes clinging to the bay-edge, and at others diverted inland of other small promontories and inaccessible areas of rocky shore.

Soon we arrive at the village of Eyeries, to be met with a kaleidoscopic assault on the senses. What a communal effort has gone on here with almost every house painted a contrasting pastel colour to the next. It is delightful to see mauve, next to lemon, next to purple next to eggshell blue, next to terracotta, and I could go on and on. We pass a church, freshly painted in cream, with the window lintels highlighted in pure white. The church has a small gable-end bell tower of the kind many a shot cowboy has fallen out of.

With the sun beating down, it's a real joy. We drove up and down to try and find the right angle to take an all-encompassing photograph, but we just couldn't find one, so we took two or three from different positions.

Continuing on our way, we find ourselves squeezed between what now must be the Atlantic Ocean to our right and the small range of hills that make up the Slieve Miskish mountains inland.

These mountains, though small and insignificant in size to many of their near neighbours, were discovered to be, in the early 19th century, copper bearing, thus the next small village we arrive at, Allihies, was once the centre of copper mining in the area. It has been recorded that over a quarter of a million tons of copper ore has passed through the smelting plants in Swansea from the mines at Allihies.

Today the village sleeps, and while not quite as compact and eye catching as the houses in Eyeries, here too, many of the properties have taken on a gaily colourful mantle. In the distance we see another feature, not overly common on the Ring of Beara, namely sand. Whenever we get the chance, we like to give the dogs a run, so we head off out of the village, down a lane to a beach. Even though it is still August and a beautiful day, the beach is deserted but for one young lad, who is exploring the boulders and rocks below a few caravans perched precariously close to the sand in a small field between road and beach.

The small golden-sanded horseshoe bay is ours and the dogs leap and whelp with joy as I open the boot. I try throwing the ball for Honey, but the sand is all soft, the tide must be quite a way in, so the ball won't roll on it. She keeps bringing it back to me and dropping at my feet, her wet nose covered in sand like a dipped Madelaine cake. Jess decides on a paddle, exploring the water's edge no further than her knees, no water lover is Jess. Honey on the other hand loves it as she now splashes past Jess to retrieve her ball which I have launched towards America. It's not too far to the end of the beach, so Angie and I sit on a rock and watch the dogs enjoying themselves. How they love the freedom! I get up and call them back, I start to throw the ball again for Honey, up the beach in an effort to get her as dry as possible before we get back to the car. Jess lies at Angie's feet, who is once more leaning back and pointing her sunglasses at the currant bun.

A few minutes later, and with the alluring miasma of damp dog assailing us from the back, we press on, windows down. We progress towards the southern edge of the ring, ready to make our way back in a roughly easterly direction towards Glengarriff.

We next see a brown sign that has us totally bamboozled. It's pointing to the right and simply has on it a motif of what can't be anything other than a Cable Car. Both utterly puzzled, but also knowing Ange to be ever adventurous, I turn to follow the sign.

Angie has more than enough adventurousness and derring-do for the both of us, so it would seem pointless for me to get involved in any of the hare-brained enterprises she's prepared to have a go at. Unlike her, I won't be Bungee Jumping any time soon[1] and I certainly won't be going over this pleasant stretch of water now before us, in what I can only describe, appearing now above me, and seemingly coming out of a garden shed, as a coffin on wires.

This was the Dursey Island Cable Car. A sign proudly announced that this was Ireland's only cable car. Unsurprisingly, it took you the short distance to Dursey Island, on which it seemed there was remarkably little to see; also, the pylons that held the wires looked very thin and Meccano-like to my frightened eye.

The Island had no shops, pubs, or cafés, and indeed a population of only four or five. This might rise to six depending on how cold and long the Dursey winter nights were. The journey across to Dursey takes about eight minutes. Just as we were mulling over whether or not Angie wanted to do it, the Cable Car, having eased out of its mooring above us, started on its way across. This meant it would be at least twenty or more minutes before setting off from the mainland again, so Ange decided to leave it for another time. I did too!

We set off again, this time headed to the town of Castletown Berehaven. Thankfully time, and maybe the cost of paint, has relegated the Haven part of the name that the

---

[1] Angie actually bungee jumped from a crane 200 feet above a Doncaster pub car park. I had a bad knee.

map so boldly announced as the road signs now say Castletownbere. We now had Bantry Bay to our right, merging with the vastness of the Atlantic it helped to fill.

The sun, now to our backs, flooded the Bay with the sort of light an artist could only dream of. The water was Cobalt blue and slate flat. A fishing boat trailed a delicate white wake, as it headed for home and, hopefully, a payday. As we approached the small town we were once again greeted to a peacock display of colours and hues.

Castletown is still one of Ireland's major fishing ports, it sits in a natural deepwater harbour and is afforded much protection by the large Bear or Bere (depending which publication you use) Island, a ten-kilometre-long and three-kilometre-wide lump of land that would fit perfectly back into the contours of the coast it obviously came from, if only someone could give it a nudge!

Castletown itself is the commercial centre of the Beara Peninsula, and though not very big, relative to other towns, here were banks and cafés, grocery shops, and numerous bars.

The goddess serendipity smiled as a car indicated to pull away from the kerb just as we were perfectly positioned to take its place.

"Fancy a beer?" I asked, not anticipating a negative riposte.

"Are you driving tonight?" she enquired.

"It's my turn," says I.

"Then why not, it'd be churlish not to," says she, opening the car door.

We wrestled the dogs onto their leads and set off up the street. After only a few yards there was a lovely-looking bar, with tables and chairs outside, more importantly it faced the sun, so the dark glasses came out and the pose was resumed. I returned from the bar with a half of what does yer good, for Madam, and a Coke for me. I was followed out of the bar by a girl staff member, who had seen us and carried an old ice cream tub filled with water for the pooches. We thanked her profusely. "No problem, aren't they gorgeous?" she said, giving each one a pat on the head as they nose dived into the tub of water.

We sat for a few moments, but the Coke just wasn't doing it for me, so I rooted in Angie's bag and pulled out the camera. "Just going for a little wander," I said, receiving the faintest of nods in return.

I ambled down towards the small harbour and snapped a few boats. I may or may not have slipped into a cake shop, I can't remember, and I took a few more photos of the bustling, colourful street. When I returned, Madam, like Lot's wife, was in exactly the same pose; the dogs side by side watching the world go by from under the table, a place I had occasionally watched the world from! From the other side of the road, I took aim with the camera, just waiting for the perfect moment when there was a lull in the traffic to allow me a clean shot. Click.

It meant absolutely nothing at the time, but just a few years later I was lying in bed, giggling out loud to one of the very best and undoubtedly funniest travel books ever written in Ireland. "We've been there," says Ange looking up from her book to the cover of mine, "the first holiday we had in Kerry; you took a photo of me and the dogs." She jumped out of bed and went straight to my sock drawer, which doubled as where we kept photos, don't ask. She looked at the third envelope she had picked up, thumbing the contents quickly. "There you are," she said, delighted, throwing a print onto the bed. It was the picture I had taken in Castletown of her sitting outside a pub with the dogs, above her was written McCarthy's Bar. I looked back to the cover of my book which showed Pete McCarthy, doffing his cap stood in the doorway of the very same pub.

McCarthy's Bar would be one of my Desert Island books, if there ever was such a programme and I was ever invited onto it. Pete McCarthy travelled much of Ireland seeking out bars which bore his name. It's a self-deprecating, intensely humorous travelogue, which records much of Ireland as it always was, counterpointed with the changing country the Celtic Tiger was bringing in. Read it; you will roar laughing!

We made our way out of Castletown, the road hugging Bantry Bay to our right, and the Caha Mountains again becoming dominant on our left, arriving at the point we had initially turned off to head over the Healy Pass. We then retraced our steps back to Glengarriff.

Though only a few miles, we decided it was too late in the afternoon to do Bantry justice, so we headed back over the hills towards Kenmare. Bantry, and other parts of West Cork, would have to wait for another day.

We stopped in Kenmare for essential supplies. Even though it's a staple, wine can be very expensive in Ireland.

As we passed the Michael J Quill Centre again, I asked, "Do you want to go out later, or have a couple before we go back?"

Ange pondered, but only for moment. "We'll go now, shall we?" she replied. "We can have a nice relaxing night in then."

"Fine by me," I replied. "The Jackie Healy Rae?" I suggested.

"Why not," came the expected reply.

The same barman was on duty as the first time we'd been in; my order and its delivery followed the same pattern as before. He arrived with Angie's lager while my Guinness was blossoming to maturity on top of the bar.

"Where've you been today?" he enquired as he laid a bar mat in front of Angie and deposited her lager on it. She regaled him with full itinerary of the day's activities. Far more information than I think he really wanted. "Still, you've had the weather," he interjected in a pause she was taking, coming up for air.

"We certainly have, fabulous," she told his back, as he returned to the bar to complete my drink.

I watched him tease the last inch or so into the glass; again, he picked up a beer mat off a pile by the pump and proceeded towards us. "It's very nice," he said, placing the mat and drink in front of me, "but not a patch on the Ring, when a ya doing the Ring?"

"We're not sure," Ange replied, "depends on the weather."

"Ah they've given it grand all week, least till Friday I'm told; do it soon," he continued. "Ya wouldn't be the first people to do it twice"

I looked at Ange. "Perhaps tomorrow," I said suggestively. Ange nodded enthusiastically, then added, "Can't wait."

"Ah tis grand, you'll love it," said the barman. "I'm a Sneem man myself originally."

"Right then," I said, theatrically rubbing my hands

together. "That's tomorrow sorted, early start, breakfast on the way."

"Grand," he said and, with that, returned to the bar.

I looked at Ange, pointing down the pub with my eyes. "There's a guy at the end of the bar, got his dog with him."

We had another beer which was my limit. Angie was happy to get back and get us and the dogs fed; so back we went up what we had already christened Walton's Mountain, had a nice tea, downed a delightful bottle of wine, and remembered we were on holiday.

CHAPTER 4

Tuesday

I CAN'T EVEN SEE THE WEEKEND FROM HERE

I was up very early, made tea for me and coffee for Madam, and took the dogs into the woods. There was a crispness to the morning, the sun not yet strong enough to prevent a shiver. The air in the woods had a freshly laundered smell, perhaps another biproduct of the lack of heat. We followed the trail our earlier expeditions had left behind, the dogs now familiar with their surroundings, checking their scent marks hadn't been interfered with by others. As always, they had managed to get themselves quite wet and grubby, so I put them straight into the car when I returned to the house.

Ange met me at the door, big handbag over her arm and dark glasses already in place. It was very unusual to get such a beaming smile so early in the morning: this Kerry air certainly suited her. She ensconced herself and her paraphernalia in the front seat while I locked up.

Just through Kenmare, before we turned onto the 'Ring' road, was a petrol station. We wanted fuel, so I filled up and moved to a parking space along the front wall. At the hot-deli I ordered tea, coffee, and two breakfast rolls. I also treated Ange to a *Pain au Chocolat*. Five minutes later we were all paid up and on the road.

Shortly after leaving the garage, signs indicated a left turn onto the N70 to Cahersiveen and advising that Sneem was 24km away. At the side of this conventional road sign was another, this was bedecked in Brown signs almost all indicating one BnB or another. They resembled the feathers on a Red Indian spear.

This road, certainly for the first few kilometres, is predominantly straight, following close to the water's edge and allowing glimpses of azure blue through the quite dense hedgerows. Where they give way to fields, stunning views across the water to yesterday's Beara Peninsula are afforded.

It's another beautiful day, we certainly have been lucky with the weather, yet again, how long can it last, I wonder. The sky is blanket blue and nearly as wide as the smile on Angie's face.

Soon the sea-views are gone, and we take a sharp right bend in the road, which is now surrounded by thick woodland, too compact to see more than a few feet into. We reach the apex of this bend and the road starts to turn back on itself. This is Blackwater Bridge. Though I notice no evidence of any such structure, it might be there, my eyes drawn to another Indian Spear of brown signs indicating much as it did before.

The hairpin loops behind us, the road now plays hide and seek with the water's edge. Sometimes we are precariously close to its shimmering blueness, then behind a rocky promontory or going through heavy woods until it again appears, so inviting. As we near Sneem, the road gets a little better, wider at least, and we pass a walled entrance way on our left that proudly announces Sneem Hotel.

Sneem, it sounds so Tolkeinian, as do many of the place names around here, Sneem the Orc? I can see that. Doesn't Killorglin sound Troll-like? Couldn't Valencia be a Princess, and MacGillyguddy? Surely a Hobbit. No?

Sneem itself is another colourful vibrant community. Hills above and beyond envelope and frame the village and its bustling centre. Already at this time in the morning there are two coaches parked around its triangular village green. Because many stretches of the road are very narrow, making passing difficult, all coaches circumnavigate the ring in an anti-clockwise direction, while cars are encouraged to make the journey, as we are, in a clockwise direction. The buildings alternate between residential properties and numerous craft and gift shops, cafés, pubs, and a bakery, which we manage to park outside. The aroma coming from inside makes me want to glide in like a Bisto Kid, but Angie is already two or three doors ahead of me, thus, answering without speaking, the possibility of a second course to breakfast. She knows me too well.

A brilliant sun illuminates, with crystal clear fresh light, the colours and shades of the houses. It is fast becoming a real pleasure, anticipating the next paint box village; I don't know how or when it started, but the fashion for colourful houses gives the area a unique coat of many colours that on a day like today really enhances the experience.

We exit the village over an old stone bridge, high above the river Sneem. The road leads us away from the coast for a few kilometres, high hills now in front and getting nearer.

Before long though, we have the sea to our left again, with

still stunning views across to the Beara. The road now travels through a very barren and stony terrain and in parts it has been hewn from the rock like a railway cutting. On both sides of the road, a jigsaw of boulders and sharp crags, set in a lush green cloth of grass, that just a few sheep forage on. The beryl, blue-green water shimmers.

Soon, cars are parked in a lay-by at the head of a track down to some golden sands. Noises from the boot suggest we are not the only ones to spot it. We find a place to pull into; on go the sunglasses and out come the dogs. We can see across the water to the end of the Beara and the vast Atlantic beyond. The beach is sumptuous, and when we are free from other users, both two and four footed, we unleash the hounds. Like a dog on fire, Honey races into the sea then turns as if to say, *C'mon, C'mon*, tail swishing like a windscreen wiper. She barks further impatient encouragement. Jess, on the other hand, just manages to dip a paw, perhaps up to the dewclaw, and that's enough, she's staying on dry land.

I look at Angie with the best sultry, sexy look I can do, I tug my belt undone and slowly drop my fly; as usual she is laughing. I let my trousers fall to reveal … my swimming shorts. Though I have no intention of going all the way in, I quickly remove shoes and socks and wade out to the ever-impatient Honey. Ball in hand, I hurl it as far as I can and she's off.

It's a very simple but rewarding joy to see one's dog so happy.

Angie wanders along at the water's edge, Jess ever present by her side. I wonder if we can get Jess some sunglasses, she really is a cool dude, unlike Honey who seems to have picked up Saint Vitus Dance somewhere along the way; she just can't get enough of the water. We travel to the end of the beach, where Angie sits on a rock and gives Jess a scratch on the head. I join her and call Honey to come out. She stands and looks at me like she hasn't heard; but when I call again, she obeys, walking straight up to where we are sat, and shakes. You'd swear blind she did that on purpose for making her come out of the water. Angie welcomes her back (expletive deleted) and we set off back up the beach, constantly shouting at Honey not to go back in the water. We want her to be as dry as possible when we get back in the car, though we both know the battle is lost in the great 'Smell of Wet Dog' avoidance stakes.

As we leave Caherdaniel, the road starts to meander; high hills pen us to the coast. There are terrific seascapes with numerous islands breaking the horizon. Small, inaccessible beaches litter the shore, golden untrod sands, so inviting as the great blue washes onto them.

We pass a sign which says Derrynane House. It rings a bell with something I had read before the trip. "Look that up," I say to Angie who is already reaching for 'Ireland – All You Need to Know' or some such named tome that we bought back in England.

"Ah," she exclaims, "it was the home of Daniel O'Connell, the Great Emaciator."

"I think that probably says 'emancipator'," I offer, "but a great man no less!"

I'm no expert on Irish history, though it does interest us both, but I do know that Daniel O'Connell was one of the first truly great Irishmen, so much so that there is hardly a town, of any size, throughout Ireland that doesn't have either an O'Connell Street, or a statue of the man.

The road continues high above the shoreline, offering sweeping dramatic views of meadows, sloping down to the water's edge; tiny croft-like farmhouses, invariably painted white, dot the landscape, like spilled Lego.

Waterville is a small coastal village oddly situated on a narrow strip of land that separates Lough Currane on the landward side of the village from the Atlantic, in the form of Ballinskelligs Bay on the other.

The seafront here is an attractive strip of grassy verge and metalled path, just perfect for a bracing morning constitutional. As you enter the village, to your left is a statue of a man who regularly took that early morning constitutional, though I doubt he wore the raggedy clothes and bendy cane his statue depicts him with. This is one Charles Chaplin, who for ten years or more, holidayed here with his family. I suppose in the late fifties and early sixties, Waterville was as far away from the world he inhabited, and yet still be able to buy a Guinness, as you could get. He stayed at the Butler Arms Hotel, an elegant hostelry, whose rooms have not only catered for Charlie Chaplin, but Walt Disney. Michael Douglas, Catherine Zeta Jones, and Michael Flatley have all stayed here, as well as a number of other notable celebrities and politicians.

We don't go in.

Waterville played an important role in the laying of early transatlantic communication cables. In 1866 the *SS Great Eastern* set forth from nearby Valencia Island, to where we are now heading, depositing telegraph cable as she went. On reaching Newfoundland, this established the first connection by telegraph twixt us and them.

We motor on, Angie is now Algy to my Biggles, navigating us towards a left turn. "Should be the next one," she says with confidence. We turn on to the R567; a brown sign indicates the Skellig Ring which confirms she is right.

The Skelligs are two smallish rocky outcrops lying off the coast hereabouts. We've seen many pictures of their dramatic shapes emerging from the sea. The larger of the two, Skellig Michael, has a 6th century Christian monastery perched towards the top of the lower of its two peaks. A couple of miles further on, I pull over into a lay-by, which is almost full with people gazing out to sea, cameras aimed at the islands. It's a terrific view, really capturing the unique shapes, particularly of Michael. Yet again we're truly thankful for how blessed we've been for the remarkable weather; I'm beginning to think it's like this every day in Ireland.

The Skelligs really are a sight worth seeing, breathtaking! On a day like this they look like something out of Star Wars, oh, hang on, they ARE something out of Star Wars, in fact, *much of Star Wars – in Ireland is filmed.*

We continue on our way, arriving at Port Magee; here the road splits, left into the village, or straight on over the bridge to Valencia Island. Signs at the entrance to the village announce boat trips to the Skelligs. On a day like today we are really tempted, but there is no way we can take or leave the dogs; besides which, Algy has other plans.

We drive the length of the island, not very far, till we come to Knightstown. "Park up," she says, I duly obey. "C'mon then, walking boots on," she says, far too enthusiastically.

Honey has heard the word 'walk' somewhere in there so she's getting excited.

"Where did you get that from?" I ask, struggling to retrieve my boots from the floor at the back of my car seat, looking at the small, folded information leaflet she had in her hand. This one titled *Walks on Valencia*. "I picked it up in that gift shop in Kenmare; there were hundreds of them."

"How many more little surprises have I got coming?" I ask from an ungainly position, trying to put a thick sock on while leaning against the car. "You'll have to wait and see, that would be telling," says she.

We set off along the road past the small jetty from which you board the small ro-ro ferry that operates at this end of the island to get you back to the mainland. A handy grass verge separates the road from the small beach area. The very narrow beach here is a mixture of sand and pebble, but easy enough to navigate, if you have sturdy boots or four feet. The sun is high above us now and the breeze running up the Portmagee channel most welcome. Ange dons her shades and I wish I had some. The glare off the water is quite blinding. Honey paddles, Jess doesn't.

I have no idea if this stretch of water is hazardous to small boats but we comment on how little – none really – traffic there is on such a beautiful day, a workday granted but the holiday season is not over yet.

"Perhaps there are very bad currents," offers Ange.

"Could be," I say. "Could be."

We walk on, hugging the shore; the dogs are in sniffing heaven.

I watch as Angie bends over to pick up a shell or an oddly

coloured or striped pebble. I think she too is in heaven; there is a beam across her face of total contentment. So utterly chilled and relaxed, it's a joy to see! This place really does have a grip on her, the land of her father. I realise with absolute certainty that this will not be our last trip to Ireland, or indeed Kerry.

We push on, the grassy hills in the distance smoky through the haze. Honey is now right in the water, just her head showing, seal-like, she barks an enthusiastic, "C'mon," but I call her out, telling her "Tomorrow babe, tomorrow." She shakes disapprovingly but plods on. A few minutes later Ange indicates where we should leave the beach. We put the leads on the dogs and walk a short distance up a lane. To our astonishment, the hedgerows on either side of this lane are made up almost entirely of Fuchsia and are utterly beautiful. At the end of the lane, we turn right to walk back into Knightstown on the same road we drove in on.

I like Valencia, it has a real charm, not *olde worlde*, but something else: it seems happy in its own skin; it's made its mark on the world and seems happy to sit back and say "We've done our bit, now it's your turn".

Its 'bit' of course was being the eastern end of the aforementioned first commercially successfully transatlantic telegraph cable, a huge endeavour which failed a few times until its ultimate success in 1866. It is also the home of one of 22 coastal weather stations mentioned in the BBC Shipping Forecast.

We arrive back at the car not a little pooped. I give the dogs a good drink and noticing that we are parked in front of the Royal Valencia Hotel. I suggest to the boss that we avail ourselves of one of the inviting garden tables and have a drink ourselves. This gets a nod of approval; so we do just that.

I order a pot of tea for one and a glass of lager for the other, I tell the bar person we are sat outside and she says, "Fine", she'll bring them out to us. In the garden Angie has donned her sunglasses and is facing the rays, the dogs have retreated to the shade that the table offers.

The waitress brings out our drinks and sets them before us; not unusually she assumes the lager is for me and puts the tea down in front of Ange. We gently exchange drinks as the waitress is now concentrating on saying hello to Honey and Jess.

"Gorgeous," she says, straightening.

"Me or the dogs?" I ask, which gets me a look from madam.

The waitress disappears but soon returns with a container full of water for the dogs.

Our thirst sated and our limbs rested, we return to the car to make the 60- or 70-yards drive to mainland ferry. This ferry is almost identical to the one we used at Passage East on Saturday; the length of the crossing is about the same as well.

Cahersiveen is busy and the plethora of pubs and cafés indicates the importance of tourism to this neck of the woods.

For those interested in such trivia, Cahersiveen has the only Catholic Church in Ireland – and there are a lot! – named after a Lay person. Namely, local boy done well, The Great Emancipator himself, Daniel O'Connell.

(That's twice I've now written Daniel O'Donnell before correcting it; they are both great Irishmen, but believe me, there is a difference.)

The road now squeezes the shore as we pass through and by Kells Bay: the wonderful Dingle Peninsula, looming ever larger over the water: in fact very shortly we arrive at a parking area explicitly to view the imposing Dingle.

"Here," she says, indicating left, so I to indicate and immediately turn onto a road that is only one car wide, and, as a consequence, has grass growing up the middle. Not something we're used to in Wiltshire. There's no point but to motor on, particularly as I haven't seen anywhere I could turn if I wanted to. Our progress is necessarily slow, praying we don't meet another car, or worse, tractor coming towards us. As we inch forward at what seems not much more than walking pace, we get the occasional flash of cobalt blue.

Suddenly, I'm driving very close to the land's edge, not cliffs, I'll grant you, but high enough for me not to want to go over the edge. But I have to stop the car, single track road or not, the view is absolutely breathtaking. There isn't a cloud in the sky, mirrored by a benevolent sea. Before us stretches the most beautiful, arced beach of golden sand you are ever likely to see anywhere. Dingle shimmers as a backdrop.

I move on, now downhill; the road also widens to incorporate a number of passing places. The odd property suddenly appears further up the hillside; one can only drool at the views they must enjoy. We can see horses being exercised in the surf along the vast beach.

We pull off the road onto a pebbled parking area. The top of the beach all along is protected by a heavy shingle strip, which is not the easiest terrain for humans or dogs to navigate, but the endless firm sand that awaits is well worth the struggle.

Honey is jumping at me like something gone mad so I fling her ball as hard as I can, it seems to roll forever, and after only two or three throws she starts to bring it back considerably slower than she chased it.

I put my arm around Angie. "You alright, girl?" I ask, I can't see her sunglassed eyes and I don't think she's crying as she rests her head on my chest and says, "What do you think?"

We walked for a good half hour then turned and retraced our steps; dogs, happy now to trot along lazily at our feet.

"The weather is amazing," I said, gazing out across the sea's silvery blue surface, where a lone boat, of some description, bobbed just below the horizon. "It can't be any hotter in Spain!"

"It's not always quite this good," she laughed.

"It is when I come," I replied.

"But it's your first trip," she laughed again.

"So?" I said. "It's always like this when I come!"

Though I didn't know at the time, this little chat turned out to be quite prophetic, for it was years, and many holidays later, that we actually had a holiday in Ireland where you could say the weather wasn't up to scratch.

A few years later we had a May holiday in Fethard on Sea in Co. Wexford, I got burnt to a crisp.

It was so nice, and the cottage so handy, that we booked to return in September. I got burnt to a crisp! We were in a pub we had frequented on both trips, Droopys, from memory, and I say to the guy behind the bar; I didn't want to ask if the pub was named after him, "What weather you get down here; we were down in May and never saw a cloud and it's exactly the same this week, it's fantastic." He looked at me and without changing his expression and continuing to dry glasses with a tea towel said: "It's not stopped feckin' raining in between." Ah well, his Guinness was first class.

Back at our beautiful beach, we threaded our way through the shingle, and gave the dogs a much-needed drink.

That had been Rossbeigh or Rossbehy beach. In Ireland such places are signposted as Strand.

The next and final stop for the day would be the very pretty town of Killorglin.

Killorglin is a very busy, bustling town, cramped with shops and pubs and cafés, but its major claim to worldwide notoriety is the famous Puck Fair. This is an annual event which takes place in the middle of August every year; we had only missed it by a couple of weeks. It traditionally involves the capturing of a wild goat, keeping him penned up for three days, and then declaring and crowning him King Puck. I'm not sure how far back this tradition goes, the cynic in me thinks it might go back to the formation of the local Licensed Victuallers Association.

Hush my mouth! I now read that earliest records suggest 1613 as a starting date. Oh, and the goat is crowned on the first day of capture by Queen Puck, usually a local schoolgirl, and again, traditionally, over the three days of its captivity, there would be a Horse Fair and a Cattle Market.

What it definitely is, is one of Ireland's oldest and best-known fairs, which thousands of people attend every year.

What a fantastic day this has been.

CHAPTER 5

Wednesday

MAY YOU FIND MOMENTS THAT MAKE YOU SMILE TODAY

Ange joined me at the breakfast table, sat down to the coffee I had passed her and, turning the open Road Atlas of Ireland towards her, asked, "Where are we for today then?" I had my back to her, buttering toast.

"Want a piece?"

"Please," she replied.

"Thought we might have a run round inland today; head back towards Macroom, then drop down to the coast and come back via Bantry. What do you think?" Her finger traced the journey I had just suggested.

"Sounds terrific," she said.

"Won't be great for the dogs till we hit the coast later, but they're well emptied," I added.

We retraced our steps of the first day back to Macroom; luckily, I found a shaded parking space. "Proper coffee, bacon butty?" I proposed.

"Sounds good," she said, so we did just that.

Back in the car, we sat and chatted for a moment or two.

Since meeting Ange and her family, I had become interested in Irish history: 1916, the fight for independence 1919-1921, the general diaspora, of which her parents were a tiny part. We already had a few books at home, but this was my first time on Irish soil.

"You know," I said, "we must be fairly close to where Michael Collins was shot."

"Beal na Blath," she replied instantly, an even keener student of Irish history than myself. I reached for the road atlas and passed it to her. "Should be on the map," I said. She opened the map to the right page.

"Should be to the south," she said, then immediately, "There," pointing at the page. I gave it a cursory glance, realised we had to continue on the N22 towards Cork, and so set off.

"Over to you, navigator," I said.

We travelled for about five or six miles, the road giving interesting views of the River Lee, which would eventually flow through Cork, and into Cobh and Cork Harbour.

She indicated a right turn coming up, which we took, and then almost immediately another right turn onto the R585. We soon arrived at a crossroads: in front of us a pub called the Diamond Bar, which rang distant bells as having played a small part in the assassination, though the mind plays tricks. I would have to look it up when we got home to Wiltshire. Opposite the pub was a small service station, and an even smaller Michael Collins gift shop. There was a noticeable lack of signage to a memorial, which I knew was at the site; so, we asked in the shop and a very helpful lady pointed us in the right direction.

We turned out of the service station to the right and followed an L road for about a mile.

Then, on the left, we came across a substantial dais, built of red brick, about three feet high. Surrounding the dais was a black wrought iron fence of about the same height, topped with decorative gold filials. Steps on the right-hand side of the monument led to a concrete base, on which stood a large stone cross inscribed with Michael Collins name in Irish. A quite large wreath and a number of other bunches of flowers, all at different stages of decay, were leaning against the base of the cross.

Michael Collins' actual resting place is at the Irish National Cemetery in Glasnevin, Dublin, where it has pride of place near the entrance, and visitor centre. His body lay in state for three days at Dublin City Hall. On the day of his funeral mass, it is estimated that 500,000 people lined the streets of Dublin, about one fifth of the entire population.

The visit had added interest for us given that we had, only a few weeks earlier, seen the Liam Neeson portrayal of Collins in the Neil Jordan biopic. As we returned to our car, two more vehicles pulled up, and five people got out, one of whom was carrying a fresh bunch of flowers.

Back in the car, I reached for the atlas. We were clearly far from the beaten track here, and I suggested to Ange we leave the next bit of navigation to the Sat Nav. She agreed, so I typed in Bandon and off we went. I almost wished we hadn't. My Sat Nav has a mind of its own and will send you through a farmyard and across a field if it thinks it can save you a nanosecond of journey time, or twenty yards less tyre-wear. I don't even know if algorithm is the right word, but whoever programmed mine was an evil little sod.

Bandon is busy. Compact streets squeeze the traffic out like toothpaste; this doesn't stop people parking down both sides of the road in some places. The other thing that hits me about Bandon is that it has, or so it seems, about a million pubs. We'd like to stop and have a walk around, but I just can't find anywhere to park that has any shade, so we promise ourselves another day perhaps, and set sail for Clonakilty.

Well, we set off for Clonakilty but the main navigator, having repossessed the road map, decides we will detour south on the R602 and head for Timoleague.

In my, shall we say, less mature years, I was a great advocate of, and if I say so myself, not the worse renditioner of, the Rugby Song. I played the game for a number of years and had acquired an acceptable portfolio of the bawdy or otherwise humorous ditties. Suddenly, from absolutely nowhere, came flooding back into my head, 'In Mobile'. This must have been because it scanned so well with the signposts I was reading that said Timoleague, so I gave it full voice and treated the navigator and the dogs to:

Timoleague, Timoleague,
Timo, Timo, Timo, Timoleague
Oh the Eagles they fly high,
And they shit right in your eye.
It's a good job cows can't fly,
Timoleague …
Timoleague, Timoleague … etc etc

"What on Earth was that crap?" came the less than positive response from the navigator.

"Just a song we used to sing after Rugby," I somewhat sheepishly replied, receiving a look that would have desalinated Lot's wife.

"I think the dogs enjoyed it," I said.

Timoleague is another pretty village straight out of the pastel paint box. It is dominated by the ruined abbey of a Franciscan Friary which dates back to the mid-thirteenth century.

It sits at the head of an inlet of Courtmacsherry Bay.

Clonakilty is one of my favourite places in Ireland and is absolutely my favourite place name. Try saying it without sounding Irish, just leave the shortest possible breath between Clona and Kilty, it's impossible. It couldn't be anywhere else.

It is a beautiful little town. Bustling and busy as everywhere seems to be, with vibrant shops and cafés with, yet again, pubs too numerous to mention. Having found good, shaded parking, we take a stroll along the main street.

"Fancy a cuppa?" I asked.

"If they sell it in halves," came the reply.

We stepped into the next pub we came to; this wasn't a long walk, you understand.

What I actually stepped into was a time capsule that transported me back, the major part of thirty years, to my best mate's front room and his ever-growing music collection.

Every square inch of wall seemed to be covered in a thousand photographs of bands and rock stars, many signed, and loads of other music memorabilia. Pride of place high on a wall was a bass guitar that was identified as belonging to

Noel Redding.

"Who?" she asked.

I knew this was going to be pointless, but I thought I'd better explain anyway.

"Noel Redding," I continued, "he played Bass for Jimi Hendrix; whenever you see Jimi Hendrix on telly on some old music programme, Noel Redding is the guy stood behind him next to the drummer, probably playing that guitar." I pointed up to the wall.

My explanation was met with pursed lips, a slight shake of the head and utter indifference.

"Tell you what," I continued with false hope in my voice, "I'll ask at the bar if there are any pubs dedicated to the Supremes and the Four Tops."

"That'd be good," she said.

I drank my coffee and left Ange enjoying her glass of cider while I went and explored the walls, nooks, and crevices of this amazing pub. I engaged with the barman who gave me the low-down on the Noel Redding connection and with the other notable musicians who had made Clonakilty their home, and this bar their home from home.

"Wow," I said as we exited the bar. "That was some place."

"Look," she replied, "there's a butchers."

This comment wasn't quite as obtuse as it might appear; earlier we had been talking about getting some Clonakilty Black Pudding for my tea.

Like the smaller Timoleague, Clonakilty sits at the head of an inlet of the Celtic Sea called Clonakilty Bay, though as far as I could ascertain the was no beach or water visible from the town itself, a short drive was required.

The aforementioned Michael Collins was schooled and lived in the town for a short while, though he was born some three miles to the west. His birthplace is now a small museum, and we were tempted, but Ange decided we needed to give the girls a good run so we made them our next priority. Navigator goggles on, she announced "Ross Carberry" and so off we set.

We travelled the few miles, with tantalising glimpses of a turquoise sea to our left, till we finally crossed the brow of a hill to be faced with an expanse of tidal estuary. Immediately before this estuary was a sign indicating Warren Strand.

Honey's keen senses had kicked in and she started with her little excited yelps, she could smell the sea from miles off. We arrived at a car park and donned our walking shoes as the dogs, well, Honey, got increasingly excited in the back.

We walked a short distance over some low sand dunes to be met, yet again, with a beautiful expanse of golden sand, a sea of the deepest blue, and a mad Golden Retriever heading straight for it. And … in she goes, barking, 'Come on in, it's great'.

Shorter than some of the amazing beaches we had already encountered, Warren Strand was nevertheless just as bonny, as we traced the shoreline to where the shallow estuary reached the Bay. We sat on some rocks near the mouth of the beach and enjoyed watching the dogs investigate and sniff their way around.

"Oh oh," said Ange; rising and retrieving a small black poo bag from her jeans pocket, she went over to where Jess had left a small deposit. We had the beach entirely to ourselves but there was no way we would have left that behind, on this or any other occasion.

The weather was yet again positively Mediterranean, so we re-walked the short length of beach, making sure the dogs were both well emptied and, Honey at least, well knackered. We retraced our way back to the main road at which point we realised that on the sea side of the road was the estuary, empty now at low tide but on the other was a lake or lagoon, full and very blue.

In front of us was the round towered corner of what we could now see was the Celtic Ross Hotel, I turned right immediately in front of it and on a whim said, "Let's have a look at Rosscarbery." We motored up the hill. We were met with a charming square of shops, pubs, cafés, and an imposing church spire that Ange had caught a glimpse of. We passed in front of an appealing looking pub whose name I couldn't make out as the front was a mass of brightly flowered hanging baskets, completely obliterating the pub's identity. We didn't park in the square but did drop down the road to look at the interesting church. It turned out to be a Cathedral, St Fachtna's Church of Ireland (Protestant) Cathedral. It was quite a mish-mash of design. A tower stood over the west end gable and then, as though an afterthought, a spire had been nestled on top of the tower. We didn't go in on this occasion, but yet again we were attracted by this pretty West Cork setting. And again, though we didn't know at the time, we would use Rosscarbery for a holiday base, two or three holidays down the line, when we could explore the town and area in even greater detail.

We soon came across the village of Leap, originally, I read,

O'Donovan's Leap, named after a local chieftain who, fleeing British soldiers, leapt a ravine near this very spot. I wonder to myself if Stan Lee ever holidayed around here.

I instigate the next detour, for just as we arrive at the outskirts of Skibb, a signpost indicates Baltimore, which is a magnetic name that just demands to be looked at, so down the R595 I turn.

I had read a little about Baltimore in my dinky book of Irish places to go and see, so thought it worth a gander.

The main claim to fame of this picturesque little village with its sheltered harbour is piracy. *Ah! Jim lad.* My little book tells me that in the early 1600s almost every woman in the village was either married to, or mistress of, a pirate. This came to an abrupt end in 1631 when the village itself was sacked by Barbary Pirates and between 100 and 200 locals were taken and sold into slavery. Today it seems to be just tourism that is catered for; the Eye-Patch, Hook, and Wooden Leg factories are all long gone.

Skibbereen is another tight and bustling small town with cars and people scampering around like mice in a cage. The main street is colourful, made more so by a proliferation of red and white checked flags of Cork. These have been evident everywhere today but for some reason seem more abundant here in Skibb than elsewhere. We slowly progress through the town and cross the impressive Ilen River before rejoining the main N71 road westwards.

Signposts now indicate that we are heading for Bantry and Bantry Bay.

I start to sing, "Have you ever been across the sea to Ireland" but am quickly advised that that song refers to

Galway Bay. "Are you sure?" I ask, she gives me another one of those looks, withering.

"Just how many times do you think I've heard my father sing that on a Sunday afternoon?" she asks.

We arrive in Bantry to be greeted by yet more deep blue water and amazing vistas over to the Beara Peninsular. On our right we pass the impressive Bantry House and gardens – perhaps another day – we press on into the town itself. Soon, hotels are abundant to our right, overlooking the now narrowing bay as it reaches the town. The main space of the town is a large pedestrianised area known as Wolfe Tone Square; at one end of which, arms extended and looking out to sea is a statue of Brendan the Navigator.

All around Wolfe Tone Square are prosperous-looking businesses, offices of administration, hotels, churches, and some exceptional homes. At the other end of the square to St Brendan is an enormous anchor. The accompanying plaque reads that this was salvaged from a wreck of a ship, of the ill-fated French Armada of 1796. This is news to me as I had no idea that a French Armada had ever been assembled. It was the aforementioned Wolfe Tone who led an insurrection in 1798 and hoped that French Republicans would help do to the English aristocracy and landowning masters what they had indeed done to their own just a few years earlier.

An invasion fleet had arrived in Bantry Bay and Beerehaven, but its efficacy in any armed struggle was negated by unfavourable wind and weather conditions. At least one of the boats sank, hence the rather impressive anchor.

Bantry was yet another of the places we had visited that we promised ourselves we'd have a better look at another time, and indeed we have.

A coffee in the sunshine watching the world go by was called for, so we did. Dogs in the shade under the table, yet again a friendly waitress brought them water to drink. I looked at Ange, "I bloody love it here!" She smiled knowingly. We sat for a few more minutes. There is something about the pace at which Ireland moves, it's chilled, relaxed, totally at ease with itself, not soporific exactly, but if I shut my eyes now, I'd be gone in seconds. Could be the heat mind you, this was our fourth successive day of cloudless blue yonder. The afternoon was pressing on, so we completed our circumnavigation of Wolfe Tone Square and headed off.

We continued northwards with the shimmering blue waters to our left. We could see Whiddy Island sleeping in the Bay mostly hidden from touristic view. Also, stippled about the bay we could see neat rows of dots. These, I was later informed, are Mussel Farms, the mussels are grown on ropes that I guess hang from these 'dotty' structures. So far, I have lived my life for more than three score years without the desire to eat any of these little shell-bound molluscs, and I'm still in no rush.

Back home, after a wash and brush up and a nice brew, dogs fed, we wandered back down to the village for a jar. I was driving again. We tried a pub over the road from the Jackie Healy Ray Bar whose name escapes me, but it was very nice. I ordered my pint of shandy and a half of lager for Ange and got into a conversation with the friendly barman.

"On holiday?" he asked as he used a twizzle stick to de-fizz the lemonade he'd poured into my glass. "Yeah," I said in my BBC newsreader's English – good guess, I thought.

"You staying local?" he asked.

"We are," I replied. "We're up at the Motor Museum, there's a rental cottage attached – hence the shandy." I nodded at the glass he'd just put in front of me. "Bit too far to walk. Well," I continued, "to walk back anyway."

"There's a shortcut through the woods," he informed me.

"Really?" I said. "But what about the river, is there a bridge?"

"'Fraid not," he continued, shaking his head, "but you can use the salmon as stepping stones." I didn't think this was as funny as he obviously did, probably because I'd rather have been picking up a nice black pint of Guinness, like the guy along the bar was doing, rather than the flat shandy now in my hand.

"What were you talking about?" asked Ange as I returned with the drinks.

"You don't want to know," I said, adding, "Can vegetarians tread on fish?" She gave me one of those looks. "I'll tell you later," I said.

We had a couple more drinks while we discussed tomorrow's expedition.

On my fourth and last visit to the bar, the barman engaged me again. He said, "If you want a decent drink, come out a bit later."

"I don't follow," I said.

"Simple," says he. "After nine o'clock all the local Gardai will be in there," he nods towards another bar, "so there'll be no chance of getting stopped!"

"Right," I said, thanking him profusely. "We might just do that."

Like hell we would!

A footnote to the above story came some years after; again, we were holidaying in Ireland when I read that the local TD for this area, Michael Healy-Rae, son of the man whose name was above the bar over the road, was in favour of loosening the drink driving laws, or, at least not further tightening them.

I'm sure Mr Healy-Rae's reasons for taking such a stand were genuine and probably had the tourist trade at heart, but it seemed an odd stand to take for someone connected with the pub industry.

All shandied out, I drove us home.

CHAPTER 6

Thursday

DON'T COUNT THE DAYS, MAKE THE DAYS COUNT

When you are on holiday with your dogs and you're looking at the map to get an idea of the day's planned journey, and you see a beach marked on the map that seems to go on forever, it's a good place to aim for. Thus, we set off, the dogs had been toileted, as had Ange, we'd had toast and coffee and were heading back to Killarney to start the day's exploration of the Dingle Peninsula, and in particular, first up, Inch Strand.

We don't see much of the village Castlemaine (I couldn't give a xxxx anyway) but cross a substantial bridge over the River Maine. I am becoming increasingly impressed by the size of the Irish rivers we have to cross, not necessarily long but many have a considerable girth. Wiltshire seems mostly babbling brooks; we do have the River Avon, but almost all of these Irish rivers seem at least as wide, if not much wider, than that splendid watercourse.

A sign welcomes us to the Dingle Peninsula and ahead lie the verdant slopes of the Slieve Mish Mountains. These are now a constant companion to our right as we progress along the R561, which soon becomes a coast road threading its way between the mountains and the sapphire waters of Dingle Bay. We are constantly afforded superb views across the water where Macgillycuddy's Reeks fill the horizon like a pointy Manhattan.

Without warning we are at Inch Strand.

We pull into the car park, at the top of which some sort of portacabin stands, about and from under which a considerable number of feral cats appear, sending Honey into paroxysms of barking madness. I suggest we make sure we put the leads on the dogs before letting them out.

Inch Beach/Strand, Strand from now on, is simply the biggest stretch of sand I've ever been on; you can't see the other end! The uncommonly wide golden littoral is backed and supported by an impressive dune system. This is a three-mile spit that stretches due south down into Dingle Bay. I notice on the road map that the impressive, but smaller, beach at Rossbeigh that we were on on Tuesday, mirrors Inch, stretching north into the bay; they almost touch like the fingers of God and Adam in the Sistine Chapel.

We walk the dogs down to the waterline in an effort to avoid the many other users already on the strand. Few seem to be swimming, perhaps the tide is going out or maybe the weather has put them off; on the horizon I can now see a proper cloud, though it is white and fluffy, and looking singularly lonely.

As subsequent visits have shown there are a lot of beaches in Ireland that you can park on, and this is no exception, cars dot the upper strand area like Dinkys on a kid's bedroom floor. They seem a long way away, such is the size of this place.

I knew from the day I had planned that there wouldn't be a lot more beach today, so we walked them a good hour. I dread to think how many miles Honey would clock up in an hour; there was a lot of long-distance ball throwing to try and dry her off a tad; even so, when we got back to the car, she looked like a drowned rat that had been dragged through a hedge backwards. Jess, of course, hadn't a hair out of place. I stood guard over the open boot as they both had a good drink of water.

We enter Dingle which is the only town on the peninsula designated as such. It also becomes immediately apparent, as we reach the dock area, that it is very much a working town. Clearly, many of the boats tied up around the harbour area are not pleasure craft. I find a shaded spot to park up for a few minutes.

The main street is full of brightly painted pubs and cafes, interspersed with a few touristy gift shops. Ange tugs my sleeve and guides me over the road into the dock area, "I want to see Fungie," she says. We cross to a quay area and walk along it towards open water.

"I don't think you can whistle him up," I said, also hoping that we might catch a glimpse. We scour the bay, hands shading eyes. Nothing.

Fungie is a bottlenose dolphin that has been living in and around the harbour area for a number of years. He seems to have taken to human company and regularly appears to swimmers or canoeists. He has become quite the tourist attraction, but on this day, there are no swimmers, no canoeists, and sadly, no Fungie. Yet another entry into the mental notebook marked 'Another Day'.

Having manoeuvred our way through the busy streets of Dingle, we took the coast road, signed as the R559 though in parts it was so narrow that an L designation might have been generous. We came to the village of Ventry where I was surprised to find another inviting strand not marked on my map. The road was narrow, winding, but stunning, the sky now again cloudless, and the views across Dingle Bay breathtaking.

We came to a lay-by on the left which allowed for, (a) more stunning views across the water or, (b) a parking area to visit some 2000-year-old Bee-Hive dwellings. I am always loath to leave the dogs in the car unattended on any day, let alone such a warm day as this, so I stayed with them, and Ange took herself off with the camera to have a look at the huts. She got back fifteen minutes later waxing lyrical about the amazingness of the little buildings. "Over 2000 years old," she said, "and not a stone missing."

If you did the journey we are on today, or in fact any of the coastal journeys we've done since we arrived in Kerry, you will notice an oft repeated sign of a white, continuous, double 'w' on a blue rectangular background. This indicates The Wild Atlantic Way and I hope whoever came up with the idea was given the freedom of Ireland and a lot of money. The WAW is a tourist route that stretches progressively for over 2500 km from the very north of Southern Ireland (which is north of Northern Ireland!), namely, Malin Head in County Donegal, all the way down the West Coast, round the corner, finishing at Kinsale in County Cork. Along this route there are 157 of what are identified as discovery points, more than 1000 other attractions and in excess of 2500 various activities to take part in. You will pass through nine counties and three provinces and see some of the most stunning sights Ireland has to offer. It is a tourist idea of Olympic Gold Medal class.

One day we intend to do it, top to bottom.

Slea Head is another fabulous place to be, on a day like this. When you stand at Slea Head you are very nearly at the westernmost point of Ireland, and by definition therefore almost at the westernmost point of Europe.

At the risk of being repetitive, it's like Groundhog Day but in a good way, the views from here are stupendous.

Offshore lie the Blasket Islands. The major island of the small group is Great Blasket Island which has remained uninhabited since 1953, my little book explains more. At its peak of population, as many as 170 plus hardy folk eked a living out of Great Blasket. The population dwindled year on year until the 1950s when as few as 20 odd people remained. About this time, a local on the island was taken very ill but the inclement weather prevented either Doctor or Priest to attend the man. He died, but the continuing inclement weather prevented his body being taken to consecrated ground on the mainland for a number of days.

This was the last straw for the few remaining islanders who contacted the Irish government and asked to be relocated.

We continued round the corner in a northerly direction and soon arrived at the small village of Dunquin. It was in and around Dunquin that many of the scenes for the 1970 film *Ryan's Daughter* were shot, which in no small way helped revive the town's economy. Another point of interest of this small village is that in Krugers Bar, in 1971 the organisation CAMRA was founded. Those who like a drop of real ale should raise a glass of it to that.

Like a lot of communities in this area, villages are more a collection of well spaced houses than a tight-knit development. Dunquin is no exception; you would be hard pushed to mark the centre. I pulled over for a leg stretch, Ange got out as well, as we enjoyed the view. Just below us in a field was a derelict ruin of I guess an old farmhouse. All that was still standing was a virtually complete gable end, which seemed odd. I reached for the camera for I could see a lovely photograph in my head. The gable had a strategically placed hole where a window would have been, this hole perfectly framed a view of the islands, I'm no David Bailey but I was quite chuffed with this little effort.

We continue to weave our way through this spectacular landscape, chaperoned as ever by the long sloping sides of hills to our right, the lower slopes dotted with bungalows and farmhouses. And to our left, more fields that occasionally give way to stunning views of the Atlantic shore.

We pass through the villages of Teeravane and Ballyferriter, sleepy in the early afternoon sun.

After two or three more miles, we come to a junction. I can just about make out the word for Dingle from the signpost but where a left turn would take us is way beyond my capacity for pronunciation. This part of Ireland is one of the few areas where, for many people, Gaelic or *Gaeilge* is still the first-choice language; it certainly is of the guy who makes the signposts anyway. As it happens, we want to head back towards Dingle, so all is not lost.

From the little I have read before coming on this trip, this afternoon's journey should be one of the real highlights and yet again the weather has delivered in spades.

It isn't long out of Dingle before you start to climb, at first slightly, a gentle incline, but in front of you are serious hills.

"We can't possibly be going over that," says Ange, looking up at the mass of hillside in front of us.

"We must be somehow," I reply, leaning over the steering wheel and peering under the sun visor. "We've got to get to the other side."

Slowly the ascent gets a little steeper; the rolling fields away to our right now seem a little more declivitous. The sides of the not too wide road are now strewn with rocks and suicidal sheep. Still, we climb. To our left the hill climbs at the same rate as it drops to our right. Ange looks behind and issues a gentle "Wow, you should see the view back to Dingle." I don't oblige, keeping my eyes firmly front facing. A small sign to the left shows a pushbike at a 45-degree angle with the message, Summit 500m. Crikey, I think, that's a long way to push a bike. Contrarily, as we near the top the road seems to flatten a little, we pass another sign indicating a viewing area coming up and, oh yeah, a Lycra-clad vision in blue, cycling towards the summit, quite comfortably it seems. We turn left into a well-appointed, low-walled car park which, surprisingly, considering the weather and time of year, is not too busy. I park at the far end where the wall gives way to a gap should people want to climb higher on foot. There are no sheep, or people, about so I lift the boot and let the dogs have a pee and a leg stretch while I fill their water bowl.

Ange has moved to an information board which tells you what you are looking at. And, what you are looking at is, yet again, quite spectacular. A great sweeping vista dotted way below with small pools, looking like sapphires in an emerald ring, in the distance, the Atlantic waits like a benign friend.

As soon as we turn left out of the car park the road changes. From Dingle we went up and over the hills; here we are clinging to the side on a road hewn out of the rock; a small low wall on our left is all the protection offered against what would be a calamitous short cut. In front, as we navigate some precarious bends, you can see where the road has been buttressed to stop it crumbling away; on our right, wherever possible, slightly wider sections have been made to provide quite scanty passing places.

After a few miles the road starts to flatten out; sheep again populate the land and there is even the odd remote homestead appearing.

"Wasn't that something," I said.

"Certainly was," Ange replied, exhaling as though the trip had exhausted her.

"What a place," I said. "What a 'kin place; how many days a year do you think they get weather like today, up there?" I say, nodding backwards. "We have been sooooo lucky!"

"Sure have," she agrees.

We pull up just short of a junction, the sign indicating a left turn to Brandon Head, Mount Brandon is another 3000+ft Irish mountain. Ange gets the map out, we 'um and ahh' as to shall we/shan't we then decide to file it in that ever-growing tome called 'Another Day'.

Before we get to Castlegregory, we see signs for Lough Gill. We are so close to the sea here that it seems odd to have a lake adjacent to it. Though I recall in an earlier life visiting Hornsea on Humberside, which had a very similar feature.

My little book of 'All Things Irish' tells me that Lough Gill is really a Lagoon, so shallow is it. Though approximately 2km by 1km, it rarely gets deeper than half a metre, so, we could walk across it, but decide not to, *not even on another day.*

Castlegregory is a pretty village with some gorgeous looking pubs, but we notice Strand Road so decide to give the pooches one last run for the day.

The beach is almost deserted, just two other cars in the small car park. I am beginning to think that a good slogan for the Irish Tourist Board could be: **Come to Ireland, there's a beach each!**

The afternoon sun is very warm, but we are very chilled.

When I say we, I of course don't mean Honey who has taken her normal position in the water and is vehemently barking instructions at me. So, I oblige Honey with a few throws of the tennis ball, while Angie and Jess enjoy a carefree saunter along the sand. This is the life; I think to myself, I could do this for a living! We walk for about 30 minutes or so, taking a dune path back in an effort to get Honey dry before we get back in the car.

Do dogs smile; do they experience happiness? It's impossible to tell of course, we've often thought that if you tickle Honey on the tum, she gives a sort of smile. It works on Angie anyway.

We followed the signs for Tralee out of the village and soon found ourselves on the main N86 Tralee-Dingle road. This is another lovely stretch of road with the Slieve Mish to our right and the blue of Tralee Bay to our left.

If mountains can be such a thing, then the Slieve Mish hills seem prettier than most. Perhaps that's an odd observation, but one that strikes me as we journey for about ten miles along their length. At the highest point they are over 2750ft, but they roll gracefully, and juxtapose perfectly with the sea.

We continue on until we reach the outskirts of Tralee, but more of Tralee tomorrow. Friday, our last day, is the only day of the week we had a definite plan for before we set off.

CHAPTER 7

Friday

IT'S FRIDAY, TIME TO GO AND MAKE STORIES FOR MONDAY

I wake to a different day. My early morning amble into the woods with the dogs is a shivery wish-I'd-put-a-jumper-on affair. There's quite a breeze blowing and a distinct lack of blue above. The three of us seemed in concert in returning to the house as soon as all necessary activities were completed.

"I think you'll want a jumper on today," I say as I hold the door for the dogs to trot in.

"Good idea," says Ange who is at the kettle preparing coffee and wearing a very elegant jumper.

"Great minds," say I.

"Fools never," says she, smiling and handing me a brew.

"You alright?" I ask. "Big day!"

"'Course I am," she replies, "I'm looking forward to it."

I sincerely hoped so; to be fair I couldn't really think of a reason why it should be any different: we were going to the home area of her father and we were going to meet a, not seen for ages, cousin, and it would be the first time she'd been back to Kerry since her father died. But, that said, he didn't die yesterday. Angie was far more stoical than one given to demonstrative emotional outbursts, but I'd keep a little weather eye on her today anyway.

Angie's father was one of those men who looked Irish. I know what you mean, it's not the same as identifying him as Chinese or say Inuit, but over the years Ange and I have always had a laugh with each other, identifying men as Irish just by looking at them. Of course there is no science here, it's just an observational thing, but we are rarely wrong, particularly when we are in Ireland. Angie's dad, Pat, died in 1992 so I'd only known him four years at most, but I always found him to be a decent if somewhat quiet guy. He liked a pint, took great pride in his appearance and smartness, and he loved his car and garden. He had a pristine lawn to the front of his house but on one of our weekend visits, the border collie bitch we had at the time, Penny, decided to take a wee right in the middle of this Centre Court quality grass. Of course no one thought anything of it at the time, but by Angie's weekly Wednesday call home we were told that this immaculate piece of God's earth looked like someone had taken a flame-thrower to it. It was one of those calls where Ange could hold the phone six inches from her ear and we could all still clearly get the drift of what was coming down the line.

To say that Pat lived his life as the subject of a despotic, dictatorial, and dominating matriarchy would be an understatement on a par with 'Bill Gates has got a bob or two'. As much as anything else, to get away from this hen-pecked existence and to grab himself five or six hours a week of freedom, Pat took up golf. So, I was asked, on our next trip north, to throw my clubs in the boot, so we could enjoy a few holes. Subsequently, I found myself on the first tee of the local municipal golf course that Pat enjoyed. Having lazily swung his driver for a few muscle-loosening stretches, Pat bent down and pushed the tee into the ground, placing a shiny new golf ball on top. A few more practice swings and then, most professionally, he addressed the ball. It sounded like he'd made good contact and I watched as his eyes followed the ball up the fairway, only to notice his head turning slightly to the right, then a little further, then further still as he watched his severe slice come to ground, just the other side of the eighteenth fairway.

"F**K," he shouted, just a little too loud I thought, and this was quickly followed by a torrent of other choice golfing expletives. I was more than a little shocked, I shouldn't have been, this man had worked underground as a coal miner, so I guessed there wouldn't have been any words he didn't know; but all the same I'd never heard him say boo to a goose.

We made our way to Tralee.

Tralee is the County town of Kerry and its administrative centre. We park up and have a walk round. One is immediately struck by the variety and class of many of the shops, and again one is impressed by the number of independent shops there are. The centre of the town has wide roads, boulevards almost – though not many – and in the centre of one stands a grand statue of a Pikeman.

This is Tralee's homage to the men who fought for Irish independence. This particular tribute is to the men who fought and died for Ireland in the 1798 rebellion. Further reading establishes that the town of Tralee, and this statue, suffered hellishly from all sides during the 1919-22 War of

Independence.

What Tralee is most famous for is the annual event known as the Rose of Tralee Festival. This festival goes some way to explaining the large number of hotels that the town enjoys. Originally, just the crowning of a local Carnival Queen, the ceremony somewhat fell by the wayside until the late 1950s when a group of local businessmen decided to re-boot the whole shebang in an attempt to boost tourism at the time of the local races.

One might say they have succeeded: the annual Rose Festival is now one of the biggest events in the Irish calendar, and the television coverage, over two nights, is usually only beaten in the viewing stakes by the All Ireland GAA finals and perhaps The Late Late Toy Show.

The affair is a world-wide celebration and Roses are chosen from the Irish Diaspora throughout the globe. Winners have come from Australia and New Zealand, the USA and Canada, and from many parts of Europe, even the UK!

A young lady from Galway is this year's winner, crowned only this week.

We make our way out of Tralee and head for Banna Strand. Its doggy heaven, and they don't mind one bit that today, for once, the sun isn't beating down with a baking heat. In fact, we have both donned fleeces as we set off on a tube-clearing walk. The strong breeze off the Atlantic filters in, salty and ozone filled. Honey's in the water, barking instructions as per usual. After a couple minutes I call Honey out and throw the ball along the beach to try and dry her off, to no avail, another day accompanied by the great smell of wet dog.

Back at the car I load them into the boot and give then a

drink while Ange makes the back seat area as tidy as possible; we may have other people in the car later. No sooner have we set off than Ange is opening her widow to the full. "Can you open the back windows?" she asks. "It stinks in here." I do as I'm told but glance in the rear-view mirror, where a great slobbering wet, white head is gazing back.

"What's she saying about you, Lummox?" I ask, and as though she understands perfectly what's going on, Honey responds with a single deep 'WOOF'!

"We need to stop and get an air freshener," says Ange, and as though in total agreement, a second loud single 'WOOF' emanates from the back.

We arrive in Ballybunion, we have no exact address to work to, only Angie's vague and hazy memory of a past visit probably twenty years earlier; but somewhere here a cousin lives. We do have a phone number if we get totally flummoxed, but Ange wants to try and find it without calling. I'm driving very slowly, Angie's eyes darting left and right like some sleuthing P.I.

"Pull over just up here." She indicates to the left where a man is in his garden. I pull over and she gets out, I hear her say "Excuse me" and then start talking to the man. At first, he looks puzzled, then his face lights up and he starts to point, leaning slightly over and moving his arm around imaginary corners. He straightens and genuinely pleased that he's been able to help. As Ange gets back in the car, he gives us a cheery, smiley wave on our way.

"Turn left in about quarter of a mile," she says.

"So who was that?" I ask, pulling away and following her instructions.

"No idea," she replies, "but wasn't he nice!"

I drive on but have to ask, "So you stopped to ask a complete stranger where Pauline lives?"

"Yes," she replied, looking at me like I was stupid. "It was difficult at first because he knew two or three Paulines, but once I'd mentioned dad's family, he knew exactly who I meant; he even said she'd be at home because she's on nights this week."

Slowly, like sunrise itself, it dawned on me that this tiny episode was the very essence of Irishness. It had taken me a week to suddenly realise why I had had such a good time but, more importantly, why I had so taken to this place. It's the oldest cliché in the book, but what attracts people to Ireland is not the wonderful scenery, not the craic that's to be had, though of course these things make it great as well, very simply, as nine out of ten folk respond when asked why they love Ireland, will honestly answer, the people. There is a tendency these days to baulk at this hackneyed and stock response, but what I had just witnessed was a perfect example of the friendliness and enthusiasm to help, and this to my mind defines the people I had encountered.

As I write this, I've lived here four years and, in that time, and on many previous and subsequent holidays, my observation from that first week has been confirmed over and over again.

We found Angie's cousin a couple of minutes later, and in no time at all we were drinking tea in her front room. After a chintzy chin-wag of perhaps fifteen or so minutes, Pauline suggested we go up to the club for a drink. At first, I was unsure what the 'club' meant but she quickly qualified this as the Golf Club. Now I was excited; if she meant THE Golf Club then it was like being invited to Lords or Twickers. This invitation was like asking a pub singer to Carnegie Hall. Not that I was going to grace the links with my athletic poise, you understand, but just to go there I thought, this would not happen in England. In 2005 the Golf Digest magazine ranked Ballybunion GC as the seventh best in the world, outside of the U.S of A.

As we pulled into the parking area, my fears of not getting in seemed justified. There were a number of long, black, people-carrier type vehicles parked at various angles. There also seemed an inordinate amount of similarly dressed, crew-cutted young men, who had bulging jackets fastened over pristine white shirts. All had a length of wire attached to their ears held in place by what must have been standard issue mirror sunglasses. In addition to these gentlemen, there were a number of people dressed in full body all-white overalls, lifting grids and dismantling lampposts and any other electrical street furniture that was accessible.

"Oh I forgot," said Pauline, "Clinton's coming, either this weekend or early next week, can't remember."

"That's that then," I said, not wishing to be water boarded in Guantanamo.

"Not at all," she said, opening the door. "C'mon." And she was dead right, out we got and up we walked to the front door, being completely ignored by everyone. In we went, and up a well-carpeted staircase, whose walls were adorned with many splendid blazered gentlemen, some I even recognised. Tom Watson faced down the stairs. On the landing at the top were action shots of many famous golfers, and this led into a bar and restaurant area.

I was fascinated, I had never been in such an august Golf Clubhouse, I walked to the great picture windows along the length of the room overlooking the course and Eighteenth Hole in particular. It was certainly some sight. The ladies fetched me a cup of tea as they got stuck into a couple of gin and tonics and continued to chat away as though I wasn't there. So I made like I wasn't and went to explore.

Fantastic action pictures were everywhere, interspaced with those of notable members and club officers. I ventured back down the stairs, I wanted to look in the Pro's Shop. I found it and, as expected, thought it a tad pricey. Some fabulous shirts and casual tops, and all at about the price of the last suit I'd bought. In a way I wasn't disappointed, the place really felt like it should be this expensive, woefully beyond my pocket ... but dead right.

The girls found me drooling, so whisked me back into the car park and the arms of the CIA. I checked the rear-view mirror a couple of times but no high-speed chase was ensuing. "I think we got away with it," I said. We dropped Pauline back off at her house and hit the road once more.

Listowel is one of County Kerry's major Market Towns and, since 2000, has been granted Heritage status, one of twenty-six towns so nominated. In Listowel's case, this is because of its architectural and historic significance. It is also regarded as one of Ireland's great literary centres and holds a prestigious Writers Week every year. Listowel also boasts a lovely racecourse that has one of Ireland's premier racing festivals, seven days on the trot in September. A few winners on the first couple of days certainly helps! Another colourful,

97

busy, bustling town: arteries clogged by traffic in this the height of the holiday season, though I suspect the narrow streets are busy at whatever time of year you visit. It looks prosperous; there doesn't seem to be many empty shops, we didn't intend to stop, but would be struggling to find somewhere to park if we wanted to.

Yet again it is a familiar feature that strikes me, this seems to be an almost daily occurrence; namely an impressive, wide, never-heard-of-before river. This time it's the River Feale, seventy-five kilometres of runoff from the Mullaghareirk Mountains and containing large populations of salmon and trout. It doesn't dominate like some rivers do; much of the town rests on the north bank, though it does encircle the racecourse. As we leave the town, we cross a substantial width of the river, now looking high summer skeletal with raised beds of stones and shrubs taking advantage of the low water level.

The road now roughly follows the course of the river until we arrive at Abbeyfeale in the County of Limerick. Here the river is the county border. We like Abbeyfeale and park up for a leg stretch and a brew. The centre of the town was dominated by a statue of a Father Casey, obviously a man who meant much to the town, so imposing is his monument. I gave the girls a drink and we found a little café just by where we had parked. We got our drinks and sat at a table by the window, Angie seemed a little quieter than usual, a little subdued.

"You alright?" I enquired. "You seem a bit fed up."

"I s'pose," she replied, "just thinking about tomorrow." She looked me straight in the eye. "I don't want to go home. I want to live here."

"It is very tempting," I said, "but I'm afraid not terribly practical just at the moment." I smiled sympathetically. "After today we don't have anywhere to live, we will have no money coming in and the car isn't ours." I'd hoped my whimsy might have lightened the moment, but, not for the first time, I was wrong. She continued to look disinterested in her coffee and the frown hadn't lifted. "Tell you what," I said, hoping to cheer her up a bit. "It's a long day tomorrow but, before we go for a beer on Sunday, I will have booked us another week over here in May. Not only that," I continued, "we'll look for somewhere next August/September time as well; won't be so bad if you know you're coming back and can count the days." She reached over and squeezed my hand on the table and gave a little smile.

"Sounds like a plan," she said. "I knew you'd love it here."

"One last look at Kenmare?" I suggested.

"Yes," she said, "I need to get some chocolates or something for the office."

"Kenmare it is," I said, looking at the dashboard clock. Late afternoon but nothing would be shut yet. One last glorious trip over the stunning road that connects Killarney and Kenmare, the Ladies View and Windy Gap, I knew this wouldn't be the last time I'd be making this journey.

I managed to find a parking space by the church and in the shade of a big tree; nevertheless, I put a bowl of water in the back with the dogs and left the back windows down an inch. The heat wasn't as fierce today as it had been for most of the week, and I knew I wasn't going to be long but it's always better to be safe than sorry.

"So," I said, locking the car, "you go your way and I'll go

mine; back here in thirty to forty minutes?"

"OK," she replied, donning unnecessary sunglasses. Off she went, at which point Honey started to throw a wobbly in the back as a lady with a poodle approached. Quite why the mildest, calmest, tamest, most gentle of dogs turns into the Hound of the Baskervilles at the sight of another dog never ceases to amaze me. Of course this only happens if Honey is in the car; if she were outside on her lead, she would let this poodle pass with barely a rectal examination. Angie says, "She's just protecting the car."

"Good girl," I shout through the window as the poodle goes by; Jess just looks at me with a pitiful WTF expression.

Ange was now out of sight, having crossed over the road and gone into a chemist's shop. I made a beeline for the gift shop on the corner that we had first visited last Sunday. I went up the stairs and made my way straight to the scarves that Ange had been lovingly touching that day. I chose the scarf she had shown interest in, a light blue slightly tartan pattern. The label said finest Cashmere from Ireland; attached to this label was another smaller one. I managed to get an attendant's attention.

"'S'cuse me," I asked, "is this little label the price, or your phone number?" She simply smiled by return, I took it over to the counter she was stood behind, and handing to her, said, "I'll take it please."

"Very good, sir." she replied. "Would you like me to wrap it?" Did she think I was going to wear it out of there?

"Yes please, if you would," I replied. "And could you put it in one of those charming plastic bags; it's got to go under my car seat for the next twenty-four hours." I retraced my steps back to the car and strategically placed it just so; hopefully it would be a nice surprise and reminder of our first trip to Ireland together.

I took the dogs out and walked them slowly up and down the pavement by the church, keeping an eagle eye out for Angie's return, I know we said thirty to forty minutes, but this meant we had at least an hour to kill.

After about an hour, Ange came stepping round the corner, to my horror she had a carrier bag from the gift shop; my heart missed a beat, but I quickly convinced myself there was no way she would spend that much money on herself. She flopped against the wall I was leaning on, and put her bag down as the dogs made out they hadn't seen her for weeks. I took a cursory glance down at the bag, but it was like a Russian doll, one bag inside another, inside another etc.

Back in the car we set off one final time, this trip anyway, back to our little cottage by the museum. We passed again the Michael J Quill centre, we'd never actually made the visit on this trip, but I knew we would be back.

We stopped in Kilgarvan one last time and, while I filled the car with diesel, Ange went in the store and bought something for our tea and a few snicky snacks for the long journey tomorrow.

Back at the cottage Ange wrote a thank you card she had bought earlier and left it with a small box of chocolates on a sideboard. I made us a brew and went outside with the dogs; I sat on a little slatted bench just outside the kitchen window, thinking of nothing in particular, when Ange joined me. We sat quietly for a few moments; then Ange said, "Well, what do you think?" I knew she meant Ireland.

"I absolutely bloody love it," I said. "In fact, I carried on, "I'm thinking about Glengarrif for May; how does that sound to you?"

She laughed. "Sounds great to me," she said and with that leaned over and kissed me on the cheek. From in front of us came a very loud 'WOOF'.

Thus ended the first of over twenty something holidays to Ireland, right up until …

PART TWO

CHAPTER 1

August 2016

HOW TO GET THERE FROM HERE …

I woke to a beautiful Buxton morning, and was just leaving the BnB I was staying in, to go and fetch my newspaper before breakfast, when my phone rang. It was a good friend and drinking buddy of mine from back home in Doncaster. Why would he be ringing me at this time?

"Woodster, what can I do for you?" At the other end of the line, all I could hear was a distraught and sobbing friend, and through his tears and anguish could just make out, "Joe's died, Joe's died last night, he just collapsed."

Joe was my best drinking chum, and very good friend, of whom both Ange and I were immensely fond; he was also Woody's father-in-law. He'd been in France, enjoying a family reunion at a sister's holiday cabin in the mountains.

Woody was clearly overwrought. "Jeez Woody I'm so, so sorry," I went on. Woody then repeated all of what he had already said, as though he couldn't believe what he told me the first time.

"Would you like me to ring a few people?" A very cracked and broken "Please" came back down the line. "OK," I said, "I'll give Donna a ring, and Dennis and Carl as well. You get back to Linds and Jayne."

"I can't believe it," he said again. "Joe's died, Joe's died."

I replied, "Get back to Linds, Woody, I'll see you later on, OK?"

A very feeble "OK" countered, and the line went dead.

I rang Angie first of course, Ange was very fond of Joe; they had always enjoyed chatting about their similar Irish backgrounds, and she was very saddened when I broke the news. Her first thought of course was for Jayne, Joe's wife, who hadn't been able to go on the trip. "God, it's so unfair," she said, "poor Jayne." I told her how broken Woody was and we chatted for a minute or so. I told her I'd promised Woody I'd make some calls, and I'd give her a ring later on at work.

Donna was the landlady of the pub where we all drank; her mum and dad lived on the same road as Joe and Jayne. Denis and Carl were good friends in our little group of drinking pals. I made the calls.

It was a dreadful few days. How else can it be when you lose such a good friend? The family had to go through the awful rigmarole of getting the body home. This leaves such a hiatus in time, not being able to have a funeral and begin the grieving process, as one normally would just a few days after departure. In the case of poor Joe, it was the best part of three weeks before we finally had the funeral service. Considering that this was late summer, the rain was biblical, which seemed to match the mood of the day perfectly. We all went back to The Wheatsheaf and drank to our dear friend. And there he was, gone!

I don't think we were actually aware at the time, but a seed had been sown. Joe's death affected us so profoundly. He was there or thereabouts our age and his death brought home just how perilous all our lives were or might be. I was driving a thousand miles a week on some of the busiest roads and motorways in the U.K. No week would pass without me coming upon yet another serious road traffic accident. As yet we hadn't discussed what it transpired we were both thinking, but it wasn't long before we did.

A few weeks later we were on our twenty-somethingth holiday to Ireland. We had ventured further abroad for three holidays, once our mortgage had finished, twice to Italy and once to Spain, but the draw of Ireland was never far away, at least twice a year anyway.

Ange had lost her mum in the January, a battling 96-year-old, and did we know it! As a consequence, Ange had met, or re-met, a number of cousins who had flown over for the funeral, and she and her sisters had been really pleased that they had made the effort. So, for this holiday we ventured where we had never been before and booked a cottage in Co. Meath. This seemed a fairly central location, where we might meet up again with those who had come over, and even see some others who had not been able to travel.

This worked well, and indeed a cousin had organised a lunch for us where we might meet other relatives of Ange, not seen for many years. We travelled to the beautiful town of

Trim, Co. Meath, and dined at a superb Golf resort complex on the outskirts of town; we had an excellent lunch and Ange really enjoyed meeting up with some long-lost cousins.

Trim is a fantastically historic place with a most magnificent castle, much used by Mel Gibson in that Scottish fantasy film he made, called *Braveheart*. The Duke of Wellington, who was Irish, born in Dublin, was the town's MP at one time. Trim should be on any Irish bucket list.

We used the week well, exploring places we had never been to before, and discovering that this particular area is drenched in history, particularly of the ancient type. At Newgrange is a prehistoric monument, consisting of a large circular mound laced with passageways and inner chambers; it is so old that it makes the Pyramids and Stonehenge look like new builds. Close to Newgrange is the Hill of Tara, another archaeological complex that was once the seat of the Kings of Ireland.

Flowing in and around both is the River Boyne, scene of a battle of 1690 between King William's Protestant forces and the Jacobite uprising of the deposed King James II of England and Ireland: remembrance of which, remains (a) a festering sore, or (b) reasons to be cheerful, north of the border to this day.

The Boyne flows into the sea at Drogheda, a place where, forty-one years earlier than the Boyne battle, Oliver Cromwell laid waste in what is regarded as one of, if not the most despicable acts of brutality ever to have taken place on Irish soil. It wouldn't be an exaggeration to say that Cromwell isn't remembered too fondly anywhere in Ireland!

We really enjoyed the week we had spent in Ireland's Historic East, and like so many places encountered for the first time, wished we had ventured this way before, having had almost all holidays in the more touristy south of the island. But let's face it, though it hardly ever rains here, we still like to chase the sun. With us of course, the dogs are always a major consideration, and life is easier and better for them if there's a beach to hand.

Talking of which, the dogs are now: a very naughty Jack Russell named Riley, or to give him his full name, Riley O'Riley; our other dog is a pure white Alsatian cross who punches first and asks questions later and goes by the rather gentle name of Bella.

If there was one thing in life that could brighten Ange's spirits, and lift her to where normal life doesn't, then it was a trip to Ireland; she was always a different person over there. This is not to say she wasn't content with our lot back home in Donny, it's just that everything went up a notch in the land of her father.

The converse side to this elation was, of course that we did have to go back to Donny, and as we traversed the M62 back towards home, there was a definite dip in both of our moods.

Ange broke the silence, "Do you think we could go and live in Ireland? I mean, would you want to; could you?"

"Wow," I said. "Let's think about that," then, after a moment, replied, "Yes, yes and yes; but we have to think long and hard about it: there's work, and the house, and money, and a whole load of other logistical stuff we'd need to get our heads around; but yes, I could live in Ireland."

Ange's face shone like that little seed was in bud.

We got back to Donny and found ourselves sitting in our

conservatory; this felt odd, as we didn't have one when we left; a splendid little addition to our home that Ange had wanted for some time. Well, here it was. It certainly confused the dogs at first, but they soon settled to its warmth-giving properties; in fact, they loved it. Once we had a Rattan settee and chairs in there, you could hardly get them out. I of course couldn't help thinking that, as a result of our conversation in the car coming home, it might turn out to be a bleedin' waste of money, but, we weren't going tomorrow; we didn't even know if we were going at all yet, and surely it would add value to the house if/when we did go, wouldn't it?

"Let's go to the Sheaf," I said.

We discussed little else over the next few weeks but our, now definite, move to Ireland. We still had many hurdles to overcome, but no matter how high the hurdle, we seemed to be able to find a reason or way to clear it. Money was of course going to be the main stumbling block: I had to be able to earn. I had decided that I might be able to make a living as a Sales Agent. A Sales Agent is a self-employed sales representative who represents a number of different companies on a commission-only basis. The beauty of it is that you can sell anything; you aren't stymied by a single product. I knew the industry I had worked in for many years reasonably well; knew a lot of the products that were sold by agents in the UK, and was hoping that a lot of these firms might not yet have ventured into Ireland.

I made inquiries of a number of companies and had had some positive responses. I was beginning more and more to like the idea of working for myself.

Another more expensive stumbling block was that I was

going to have to buy a car. In my life I had only ever owned my first car; all the rest being company cars. That we were able to undertake a move to Ireland at all was largely down to a small legacy Ange had received after the death of her mum, and we decided to put aside at least £7000 to buy a car nearer the time.

What we had to do next was give ourselves a timetable and prioritise a list of the jobs that had to be done. The first decision we had to make was 'when'? We thought long and hard and decided that I needed to build a portfolio of products to sell; and if these were going to be predominantly in the Cycle Industry, where I had worked for many years, then I needed to be in Ireland for the start of the summer, so I could hopefully hit the ground running. We arrived at the idea of being in Ireland by the end of June 2017. We then needed to decide when to tell my present employers of our plans. We decided I should give them the best part of six months' notice, and so I would tell them at our Christmas party down in Birmingham.

The next few weeks and months saw us thinking about, and talking about, nothing else. Our lounge was a monument to all things Irish. Maps of every type, everywhere; information about each and every county. The world, or at least Ireland, was our oyster and the big question we had to find an answer to was: where to live? Common sense finally prevailed, and even though Ange had imagined for years what a dream it would be to live in County Kerry, we both understood that it was hardly in the middle of the country; and as I was going to be travelling to all compass points, it was necessary to be situated somewhere in the middle.

We both knew that the endeavour we were going to embark upon was a bit of a gamble: we weren't penniless but there was no way we could do this without my earning money. To this end, we decided that we would not sell our property in Doncaster, but rent it out for twelve months, while we rented a property in Ireland for the same period. The idea being that we would know within the year whether or not I was able to make a go of it.

There are many delightful things about Ireland that make you chuckle; one of which became apparent now as we started to look for properties to rent. The catch-all website when looking for houses to buy or rent in Ireland is called … DAFT.ie, I kid you not!. I have no idea if DAFT is an acronym, I assume it probably is, but it's a wonderful thing that whoever thought it up saw no problem in using it.

It seemed obvious that I needed to narrow the search to just four central counties, namely Roscommon, Longford, Westmeath, and Offaly. Each day I would come home from work, straight to the iPad and search, search, search. Ange of course put me right when she said, "What's the point of doing that now, you'll end up finding something brilliant that we can afford, and what're you going to do then: ask them to hold it for seven months? You don't need to even look at DAFT until at least the end of March/April time." It was really difficult not to, and so of course I didn't stop. I still looked every day even though I couldn't let on; else I'd get one of those withering looks. My covert exploratory searchings had determined one thing though: when it was time to look, I was going to concentrate on County Longford/County Roscommon.

We were in the front room sometime later when I said to Ange, "Do you think we should change the May holiday, and try and go somewhere nearer where we need to be?"

"By then we should have found somewhere," she replied.

We had a long-standing booking for a cottage on the Ring of Kerry for May the following year; it would have been awkward to change it, as well as expensive. For some years now we had taken my widowed brother Charles with us on our May holiday; he probably wouldn't have minded if we did change it, but he has a penchant for looking at mountains, and Kerry is right up his street.

So we found ourselves in late September, in possibly the autumn of our own years, planning and talking about what is quite a momentous decision for a pair, nearing retirement, to take. We chatted about little else privately, as we swore ourselves to secrecy until at least my notice went in; even then we decided we might hang on a bit, because all we would get was question after question that we could not at that point answer.

The next few weeks were slow; true it was helped by being the busiest time of the year for me work-wise, but all I could think about as I traversed and criss-crossed the north of England was the middle of Ireland. We had an almost daily delivery from Amazon, as every possible book or map arrived. We both started reading Irish thrillers, so immersed were we in our adventure. Angie's interest in Irish History had already stockpiled quite a library of books of that ilk.

We did start to declutter a little by showering various charity shops with more than 400 paperbacks we had managed to gather since moving to Doncaster. I'm not a great fan of lugging Tea Chests of books around when moving. We would be making an exception for the Irish ones though. My many beautiful, and much loved, reference books would present another problem nearer the time. And what about the Wisdens!

The day of my work's Christmas dinner approached. Was I nervous? Not a bit, I couldn't wait, it would be like a starting-pistol going off. The company I worked for were owned and run by a Taiwanese family, and as God is my witness, a person could not wish for better or nicer people to work for. The two senior people at the company were a brother and sister, not very old at all, though I am getting to the point where far more people on the planet fit into that category than into the one I'm in. The third member of the family was the sister's husband who was responsible for purchasing, and he was just as decent as the other two.

When I say Christmas dinner, I use the term generically; every year we went into China Town in Birmingham and were treated to the most lavish spread of Szechwanese loveliness that it is possible to imagine; just to walk in the place made me drool like Homer Simpson!

I was seated at one of three large round tables that took the entire company staff. One of the lovely things about working for this company was that there was absolutely no hierarchy; by which I mean, after the three Taiwanese people, who had total control and responsibility for the business, we were all the same: sales, accounts, warehouse staff, cleaners, all sat round the same tables, no pecking order, no empire builders, no one person more senior than the next. Brilliant! I've worked at companies where people would have slit throats to be seated near the bosses; not here, not a bit of it.

As you can imagine, this was a company very few people ever left, or wanted to leave. This was particularly true of the sales team, where there had been hardly any turnover of staff in the fourteen years I had been there. The odd retirement – I think, one replaced for being a little naughty, and one whose area was the whole of Scotland, but who put weekly reports in showing mileages of such small number it was fairly obvious he hardly ever left Glasgow!

I waited until people had finished eating and were mingling with one another, some at the bar, some looking through Karaoke songbooks, and found an empty seat next to Tony, the boss.

"Tony," I said, "firstly, thank you for that gorgeous spread."

"OK," he replied, nodding; he had the most endearing way of saying OK, the K would be elongated to at least two seconds long.

"Secondly," I continued, "Angie and I have decided we are going to go and live in Ireland."

"Irand." He looked a little surprised and then with at least a three-second K said, "OK …"

That's enough of trying to write in the Chinese vernacular. He asked me when, so I told him with a smile that I was effectively giving him six months notice. He smiled back, "OK." We talked a little more, but he suggested I pop down to Birmingham in January when we could sort out what needed sorting out then.

I called Ange the next morning from the car on my way back up the A38.

"That's it," I said. "Jobless, no turning back now."

She laughed, "Better pull your finger out and find some work then," she continued, "I'm retiring."

We had a chat about the evening and how it had gone; she was always invited to go but it would mean putting the dogs away for just one night, and that always seemed more trouble than it was worth.

"I've got a present for you," I said.

"Oh good," she replied, "how much?"

At the company Christmas do, everyone was invited to choose an envelope by lottery. There would be a bag with a piece of paper with everybody's name on it; someone would pick a name out and then that person would get to choose an envelope that had been fanned out in front of them, like a magic trick. Every envelope contained at least £50, so no one went home empty-handed. A couple or three of the envelopes would have £100 in them, and one – might have been two – would have £200 in them.

I walked through the door with my little bag of goodies from the night before, Ferrero Rocher, Christmas cards, perhaps a calendar, crackers.

"Envelope," she said, holding her hand out. "Envelope," flicking her fingers towards me.

"Nice to see you too," I said, pulling a doubled envelope out of my jeans back pocket.

I passed her the envelope and gave my attention to two frantic dogs that were leaping at me. "Someone's pleased to see me," I said.

She removed four £50 pound notes from the envelope.

"Well done," she said and moved to kiss me, though not as enthusiastically as the dogs, it has to be said.

"A nice bit of spending money for Lismore. Michael will be pleased," she said.

The one place above all others that I/we had fallen in love with in Ireland was Lismore, in Co. Waterford, and we were going to spend Christmas there. A little further from the sea, 17 miles, than we usually pick, but I was enraptured by the place from my first ever visit.

The best way to approach Lismore is from the east; you pass through the pretty village of Cappoquin, and then follow the valley of the Blackwater River for about six kilometres. The road hugs the wide, impressive river, until suddenly you arrive at a view, quite Disneyesque. That is to say, what you actually arrive at is the stunning vista of Lismore Castle, sitting high on a bluff above the river, as imposing a castle as any in Ireland, and there are plenty to choose from.

Ireland has a wonderful volunteer organisation called 'Tidy Towns'. Every year since 1958 there is an overall winner, this is a truly great achievement and a marvellous accolade to those involved.

In 2002 the awards were divided into three categories, Best Village, Small Town, and Large Town; the overall winner would always be one of these. More on Tidy Towns later, but I mention it here because, from the first year of the new categories, Lismore has won the Small Town award on five occasions and was awarded the overall crown in 2004. It really is a lovely place.

I was seeing this fabulous vista for the umpteenth time as I drove into the town for our Christmas break. Ever since we had won the lottery – not really, but we had finished our £700-a-month mortgage, so it felt like it – we have been to coming to Ireland for Christmas.

Of course, on this trip, we were looking at everywhere, and everything, with fresh eyes. Trying to take in, and to comprehend the subtleties and nuances of Irish life; something we intended very soon to become a part of. Everything on this trip, our first since deciding to move, would resonate with a slightly different importance and meaning. We would be trying to see not with the eyes of a tourist, but those of a resident.

Michael was the landlord of a great little pub, at the crossroads in the centre of town, called The Red House. There was nothing extraordinary about the pub, but great beer and a friendly welcome was guaranteed. This is exactly what we received as we walked through the door and Michael spotted us, beaming, as he came from behind the counter to shake our hands. Pleasantries over, we sat down to enjoy our first beer of the trip.

We hadn't been to Lismore for two years, and it was a joy to be back. Last Christmas, (bursts into Wham song) we went to Duncannon, the first place we had stopped on our very first trip.

Christmas Eve in Duncannon was a cracking night, typical of pubs all over the UK and Ireland, it was full of those who had left home, but had returned for the holidays. The two pubs in the village were no exception, and a great night and lovely atmosphere ensued. The following morning, Christmas Day, we stepped onto the beach, our cottage was that close, to walk and run the dogs to the point of exhaustion. A bright, crisp, invigorating morning though a tad on the chilly side. We walked a long way, to the far end of the beach, a good distance for me. As we meandered our way back, a few other parked cars were letting loose the family hounds, having the same idea as ourselves. It was so very friendly, 'Happy Christmas', and sparkling new jumpers, echoing all over.

A few yards from where we had walked onto the beach, there were some steps leading up onto the road; we took these so we could deposit the little black bags Ange was carrying into the bin that was at the top. Job done, we started back the hundred or so yards to our cottage.

At this point a chap emerged from a house to our left, I recognised him straight away as the Landlord from the pub we had spent most of the previous night in, which was directly over the road. I later discovered that his mother lived above the pub, and he and his family in this house. He called to us, in his hand was a parcel of tin foil. "Saw you walking round the beach," he said, "thought you might like this." He handed me the parcel, "Just a bit of Christmas cake. Merry Christmas," and with that he turned and went back into his lovely home.

Ireland, eh!

Back in Lismore, we managed over the next few days to sit down and have a chat with Michael about our plans. He was obviously excited for us, but, at the same time, concerned we were actually going to take this plunge with our eyes open. He asked me to remind him of the area I now worked, I told him it was roughly thirty miles either side of the M62 from Hull across to Liverpool in the north of England, then further up each coast as far as Newcastle in the East and Barrow in

Furness in the West. I added, I also do North Wales.

"So as far as big towns go?" he asked.

I replied, "Well there's Hull, Hell and Halifax, Sheffield, Doncaster, Rotherham, Leeds, all those other Yorkshire towns; then I've got Greater Manchester, Liverpool and all of Merseyside, and all those other Lancashire towns."

He looked a little serious. "You do know," he continued, "that the entire population of Ireland will probably be only a little more than Manchester and Merseyside combined, and that a quarter or more of those will be in Dublin?"

I had never once considered this matter of size and scale. I would be having a whole country to rep and, at the same time, downsizing considerably. I didn't know what the population of Ireland was, I'd never given it a moment's thought, or, if I did know, it hadn't registered. It was a little sobering to say the least. "I don't want to put you off, because I know how much you love it here; but you must make sure you do your homework." He paused. "Now, what're you having?"

Michael's little chat was a reality check at exactly the time we needed one. To be fair, we had been gushing about how great everything was going to be; how easy! Michael had confirmed to us one thing, that we were right not to sell our house, but rent it out for twelve months, and do the same in Ireland. Worst case scenario, if we had to come back, I might not have a job but at least we would have somewhere to live.

Of course it didn't put us off one bit, but it did make us a little more circumspect when considering all that we had to do.

On the drive home from a wonderful Christmas in Lismore, we considered a timetable. Ange had a pad out on which to make notes. We discussed when we were going to tell anyone, and decided not to, before we had somewhere to live. Which might be giving two months notice to friends and family, no more. We were prepared to pay perhaps an extra month's rent before we got there, if it secured an ideal property. Ange handing her notice in would be a straightforward month's notice, I suggested she make sure she had at least two weeks off in Donny before we left. I would give Tony a ring at the office, as soon as he was back from his Christmas Taiwan trip, and arrange a meeting; things might become a little clearer after that. We noted that we would have to find a removal firm that operated between the two countries. Also, I would need to start looking for a car; we did have space on our drive if the right vehicle came up, before the company car went back. We started what was to be a momentous New Year, like a couple of giddy school kids who know a secret but have promised not to tell.

In the middle of January, I travelled down to our head office in Birmingham for the promised chat with Tony, Amy, and Oliver. We had a natter, where I outlined what our intentions were: what I was proposing to do, as a Sales Agent; who else I had spoken with, my plans to buy a car, when Tony dropped a bombshell.

"Why don't you work for us in Ireland? We have been thinking about getting a presence there, but were unsure how to do it, this could be a way."

I was seriously gobsmacked. "Wow," I said, "I did not see that coming." I couldn't say anything much for a second or two. Oddly, my most pressing thought was that I wanted to work for myself, not continue in paid employment. "Wow," I said again, trying to compose a response, when Tony added, "You wouldn't be working for us directly. Still an Agent, but we would only want you to sell our products, no one else."

One of the others said, "We will pay you a retainer, this can help towards petrol costs etc, and of course a commission on top."

This was all somewhat overwhelming, after a hundred little chats with Ange about this product or that one, about how much we could subsidise our lifestyle from savings until I could earn proper money. The lovely people that I worked for were just making the whole process simpler, and were, without doubt, easing our passage both workwise and financially. "Wow," I said for the third time. "Obviously I will need to go and chat with Ange, but I can categorically tell you that the answer will be yes, yes, yes."

With the meeting finished, we all took a sort of collective sigh of relief. I was asked my plans for a car, so I told them my budget. We touched on a timescale for the move. All I could reiterate was early summer, hopefully. We would have to find a place to live and would probably start looking around April/May time. "Then it will be all systems go," I said. "We are booked to go over in May on holiday, so hopefully we might have something in place by then, that we could firm up on while on that trip."

We agreed that we wouldn't announce my plans to the rest of the company until a later date; we also agreed that further meetings would be needed to agree a contract, commission scales, price levels etc. All I really wanted to do now was tell Ange. I called her from the car park before setting off; she was clearly as excited as I was, but her enthusiasm had to be stymied a little by the close presence of colleagues. "OK," I said, "you can get proper excited in the 'Sheaf later on."

In the 'Sheaf later on, we were contemplating just what change Tony's offer had made to our plans; it had blown them apart really, primarily of course in the question of money. I clearly wasn't going to be offered a full salary, but I was certainly going to get the help I needed to establish both myself and the brand. This was such a relief; the main pressure point of the whole enterprise had been alleviated.

"We need to do a recce," I said.

"What do you mean?" she asked.

"I'm thinking a few days in Dublin; we can visit a few shops, get a feel for the business over there, see where our products might fit in. It'd give me a much better idea when I go to Birmingham for the next meeting."

"Makes sense," she said. "When?"

"Soon as," I replied. "I'll just have another Guinness and we'll go back and see what we can do."

What we could do was book a four-day trip through Stena, on a very reasonable out-of-season package, January/February clearly being the quiet period. We got an all-in package in a really nice city centre hotel. What was even better was that when I told Tony of my plans, he offered to go halves on the cost.

So, this is exactly what we did. We parked the dogs in the local kennels and set off back to Ireland at the beginning of February, barely six weeks since our last visit.

I visited a number of shops in and around Dublin, showing then our current catalogues and getting a positive response from most. I had arranged a meeting with a Dublin wholesaler, to get a feel from his perspective; he was less positive than the shops, but not enough to put me off.

We spent one day travelling into the country, to view a property I had seen on DAFT. This was some way out, and quite probably not central enough for our plans, but it was travelling to an area we hadn't been to before – always interesting – North Tipperary, and the name of the village, Horse and Jockey (I kid you not), intrigued me. As it happens, we got to said village and could not find the property. We asked in the local shop, even showed a picture of it off the iPad, but no one recognised it, or could tell us where it was. Still, it was an enjoyable day out.

On our return to England, I hastily arranged another meeting in Birmingham so I could disclose and discuss what I had learned regarding pricing levels, and where our products might fit in etc. The meeting was very positive, and I was even made an exceptionally generous offer to buy my company car, if I so wished, and I wished.

Ange and I had thought long and hard about a departure date, our plan was to move in May, but a number of factors came in to play that determined June would be the better bet. It would mean I was losing a good few weeks of the selling season, but realistically I wasn't going to pull up any trees in those first few months. We also decided that to make things more helpful to Birmingham, I would leave on pay-day, so the date was set for my last day of work in the UK, to be 21st June 2017. We would arrange to leave for Ireland the following week, so that our house might be marketed as occupiable from 01/07.

It was now March/April and finding somewhere to live in Ireland became a more pressing concern. I concentrated my DAFT exploration on three places in particular; these seemed to have a few, though not a lot, properties available. Actually, properties to rent were really quite scarce.

The Strokestown/Roosky area of Roscommon had a few that were interesting, and there were a number in Longford town, but the area that appealed the most, bearing in mind we had never been anywhere near any of these places, was the small town of Lanesborough/Ballyleague. So good they named it twice!

The River Shannon runs through its centre, not only splitting the place between Co. Longford (Lanesborough) and Co. Roscommon (Ballyleague), but also provincially. Longford being in Leinster, and Roscommon a county of the Province of Connaught.

I found what looked like a suitable bungalow, though for appreciably more money than we wanted to pay; it would mean we would have to subsidise our monthly rent from savings, as it was quite a bit more than we would be receiving for our Doncaster home. However, we were fast getting to the point where we had to say yes to a property so we could start to make other plans, like organising home removal, and ferry tickets (one way!), so we bit the bullet and contacted the agent for the property, telling him we were interested.

Somewhat serendipitously, on the Saturday, at the end of our forthcoming May holiday to Kerry with brother Charles, it was Ange's sister's 60th birthday. Ange's sister lives in Ballycastle, a very pretty place in Northern Ireland. The journey we would have to make was just about as long a journey as it is possible to make on the entire island. Caherdaniel on the Ring of Kerry, to Ballycastle, must be over 600km, almost 400 miles, with the slight detour we planned; this was turning into a busman's holiday for me. What it did do, however, was allow us to plot a course where we would be able to visit the bungalow in Lanesborough, about halfway through the journey north. This we did.

I had made arrangements to meet up with the letting agent at the property on the Saturday lunchtime. We made good time and managed to find the bungalow without a problem; the Agent met us there and showed us around. It still needed a little work to be done, a wood floor was being laid throughout the hallway and the entire house was enjoying a lick of paint. On the downside the back garden was an absolute jungle, and unless the owners were prepared to do something about it, it was going to be totally out of bounds and useless, even for the dogs! The front of the property had a large lawn, and ample parking.

I could tell Ange was a little disappointed, the kitchen hadn't changed since the sixties – since it was built even – and we would be cooking using a gas cylinder, something neither of us had ever done. The kitchen floor was also unsatisfactory, and we asked the Agent that something be done about it; he agreed it was unacceptable. A new Linoleum type floor was laid before we moved in.

I had advised the Agent that, so as not to lose the bungalow, we would pay rent for the month of June, even though we would not be moving in until the beginning of July. To his credit he said this wouldn't be necessary, as the bungalow might not be up and running by then anyway, and so would start our contract from 1st July, as agreed.

I must admit we left for the North feeling a little dejected; we were paying a lot of money for a property that wasn't a patch on our own, for which we were receiving considerably less. It's impossible not to feel a little disheartened at this prospect, however, we soon came round to the idea that our own furniture, and the dogs etc, would make it a little more palatable; and it certainly wasn't for ever, 12 months max.

We enjoyed a most surreal night in Ballycastle, which included the sight of my sixty-year-old sister-in-law belly dancing in full eastern garb with a group of other women, mostly of a similar age, who should all have known better; but we had a good laugh.

Having made our way back across the Irish Sea, it was now time to really buckle down and start dotting the i's and crossing the t's for our forthcoming adventure.

Ange had a lot of fun dealing with a removal company based in Nottingham. Having to forward inventories and the such made us make decisions on what we were going to take with us and what was going to the skip/charity-shop/bonfire. I booked our one-way tickets from Holyhead to Dublin.

We decided to go a few days before we could take possession of the bungalow; this meant finding a hotel within an hour or so's drive of Lanesborough. This was harder said than done, taking into account we would have the dogs with us, but eventually we found a decent hotel in Kiltimagh, Co Mayo, which served its purpose very well indeed.

As we approached our final week in England, I had said goodbye to all my customers, many of whom had become good friends over the years; I received a number of small gifts (bottles), and from one customer in particular, a beautifully engraved, glass tankard. A touching thank you for my help over the years. It was all really poignant, not one good riddance, at least to my face anyway!

I went through the usual leaving-ritual down in Birmingham, which was a little odd really: I would still effectively be working for the company, though not on its payroll. They were as generous to me as they had been all along, and I was presented with some gorgeous cut-glass champagne flutes, and, of course, a good-sized bottle of fizz to go with them.

Back home we had just two or three days to blastoff.

I mentioned that Ange had had some fun booking the removal men. When they eventually turned up, and introduced themselves, I knew we were in for a laugh. The main man was the only person I had ever met who drank more tea than I did and was he ever one for a story!

He told me this tale of a lad he had taken on, back in Nottingham, a few years previously.

"Best bloody worker I've ever had, didn't speak a word of bloody English, but boy could he shift bloody furniture, and strong as a bloody Ox." He carried on, "Wife was Latvian I think, a senior nurse, and she spoke good English, he was Latvian or Russian, or summat, but couldn't pick the lingo up at all, barely a word. Anyway, he handed 'is notice in 'cos his wife got a promotion, but it meant they had to move to Derby, so he couldn't work for me anymore," he laughed because he knew what was coming. "Anyway, on his last day I said to him, 'I know you haven't picked up much English but what's your favourite word of those you have?' Obviously I had to say this in the very stilted and hand gesturing way that we managed to communicate in, he thought for a moment, in fact, I didn't think he'd understood the question, when he suddenly said ... 'Bungalow'"!

GONE WEST

How could I live without,
That early morning fix,
Of news, and sport, and weathermen,
Of deceitful politics.

A constant hum for many years,
As I drove about my work,
He says this, she says that,
Clouded in the murk.

Truth, it seems came secondplace,
A disregard of us,
People believe what they want to believe,
Oh! That stupid bus.

On it went and on and on,
Every morning the same,
No one knowing what that the answer was,
But all knowing who to blame.

How will it end, still no one knows,
We'll have to wait and see,
Me, I've already decided,
I'm across the Irish Sea.

My mornings now are full of time,
No rush to be elsewhere,
No ranting, raving politicos,
Using up my air.

It's the gentle hum of silence now,
That wakens me from sleep,
The noiseless peace of an empty mind,
Beside the Shannon deep.

Oh, I can live without that fix,
Most certainly I can,
To no more drown in politics,
That is the promised land.

PART THREE

CHAPTER 1

THE POSTIE, AND THE MAN WITH THE VAN

We departed our hotel in Kiltimagh, having had a very pleasant few days in lovely County Mayo, getting to know yet another beautiful part of the country. Stunning mountains, countryside, and beaches. We felt suitably revived and refreshed, and on the big day up early, so we would be in Lanesborough in good time for the arrival of our furniture.

It wasn't lost on us that this was a monumental day, the first of the rest of our lives. Ties to the UK, ninety percent severed, we really should have been perhaps more apprehensive than we were; instead, we both enjoyed a feeling of excitement that was almost childlike.

Our first port of call when arriving in Lanesborough was at the garage at the top of town; the house agent had arranged that he would leave our keys in an envelope behind the counter. How Irish!

We also needed diesel, as well as a few other basics, tea, coffee, milk and, knowing who was coming, probably more tea! Angie joked as I was stepping out of the car that we'd have to find the box with our kettle in first.

As I was filling the car, a postman stepped out of his van,

this was parked to the side of the forecourt. He started to walk towards me, in his hand a bundle of letters etc, wrapped in a plastic bag, and secured with a rubber band.

"Andrew Knowles?" he asked, approaching my car.

"Yes," I replied, taking an indiscernible step backwards.

"Thought it might be you," he continued. "You moving in today?"

"Yes," I again replied, as he handed me the package.

"Great," he said, "I'm Louie, I'll deliver your post daily from now on then; nice meeting you," and with that he turned away and went about his business.

I looked open mouthed through the car window at Ange.

Inside the garage shop I couldn't get the newspaper I wanted and was advised of the licensing regulations with regard to the sale of alcohol. They didn't sell it anyway, but I was told I could get it after 10.30 a.m. from Supervalu, our local small supermarket just at the other end of town. To this day, the off-licensing regulations in Ireland dictate that you cannot buy alcohol before 10.30 a.m. on a weekday, and on a Sunday not before 12.30 p.m., even though the pubs have been open since noon, or, in some cases, since breakfast …

We made our way down to the bungalow, perhaps a kilometre from the garage. On opening up, we saw that, as promised, a new wooden floor had been laid throughout the hall area, and a new sort of linoleum-type covering on the kitchen floor.

Only twenty or so minutes after the *eta* our furniture remover had given us, the big van pulled up just beyond our front gate and started to reverse into the driveway.

"You'd better find the boxes marked kitchen first. If you want a cup of tea, that is," I joked with the driver as we cordially shook hands, and briefly discussed the crossing they'd had.

The requisite box was soon found, and the kettle put on. The rest of our worldly possessions were soon decamped into our new, albeit temporary home. Boxes, all clearly marked, were placed in the relevant rooms, and more tea and biscuits were taken.

All this time Bella and Riley had been going frantic in the back of my car, and I was desperate to let them out to explore their new home. So, after a final brew, we shook hands with the removal man and his assistant, slipping them a €20 note for their trouble, and bade them a safe trip back. We waved them off as the van edged out into the road. At last, I let the dogs out, noticing immediately that the rear window would have to be cleaned, so smeared inside was it with doggy nose marks. Though, as the light caught the window, it struck me that the dogs had made a right Jackson Pollock of it, and so toyed with presenting it *fait accompli* to the MOMA. Could be worth millions, I cleaned the window …

Surrounded by boxes, and with hours of work ahead of us, we decided it was necessary to prioritise, so, we determined that the best and most helpful thing to do would be to go and check out the local hostelries. It was a twelve-minute walk into town, often a little longer back!

Having been to Ireland many times, we were not surprised that such a small community would have four pubs. Three of them were in a good darts throw of each other, and for absolutely no reason whatsoever we decided on a bar called

Clarke's. There were only two people in the bar at the time and, despite them both being Manchester United fans (and believe me, that's not a minority faction in Ireland), they have since become friends.

CHAPTER 2

BECOMING IRISH, HOW HARD CAN IT BE?

We needed to get a grip and make sure we had the essentials of life. We made tentative inquiries about getting Sky, and having an Irish mobile phone account and number, but it soon became evident that before any of that can happen, what you have to have is an Irish bank account.

The house agent recommended the bank he used as he was a neighbour of the manager, and as we had not a clue in comparing one bank to another, and, as it was just about the nearest bank to the main car park in Roscommon, so this is the bank we chose.

We first attempted the direct approach of queuing, only to be told we couldn't open an account with a teller. It had to be done, by appointment, with another member of staff, and an interview would have to be arranged. This was a bit of a bugger, because this was Thursday and we couldn't get an appointment before Tuesday. We tried other banks, but the waiting time was just as long, so we went back to the first bank and made a date for the next Tuesday.

Now, it doesn't take much to get me started on banks, they are run like no other business on the planet; they take your money without asking and charge you without invoicing. They constantly change their IT systems, and then spend millions on advertising, telling us it's for our benefit, when we all know it's actually for theirs.

(The problem they actually have is keeping their huge IT Departments happy; these are great to have if your IT goes down, but when all is running smoothly, what do they do? I'll tell you what they do, they fix things that aren't broke!)

No matter how busy the bank is, or how long the queue of people waiting to be served, there will always be a ratio of 1 to 4 of tellers, to those doing other things in the background. I defy absolutely anyone to admit to seeing all the cashier positions open no matter how busy the bank was.

Some months later I was waiting to pay some money in at a branch in Longford town. It was lunchtime, and the bank was rammed, and the queue, no exaggeration here, was outside the door. This after a considerable snaking queue inside. There were two teller points open, but one of the tellers was dealing with an obviously involved enquiry, which effectively meant there was one cashier point in operation; two teller positions were closed, and as ever, there were a number of people doing other things and milling around in the background.

At this point, as I queued patiently, I imagined the Bank's Business Adviser paying a visit to my imaginary shop. When he arrives, there are loads of customers, all queuing with goods in their hands that they want to buy. There are four till points on the counter but only one is occupied, but other members of staff can be seen, doing paperwork in the background, or restocking shelves, or drinking tea. The customers are starting to get fed up, some are returning their purchase items back to the shelves and leaving without buying anything.

The Business Manager takes me to one side after the customer rush has subsided, and in no uncertain terms tells me that what he has just witnessed is poor business practice. Not only was I losing customers, but I was definitely losing goodwill. There is no point, he went on, in having four till positions, if they aren't used by staff when you are that busy.

Of course, any shop that behaved in the way my imaginary one did, wouldn't be in business very long.

Banks eh!

We were OK for shopping, and getting cash etc., as our English cards all work perfectly well here, but we needed an Irish bank account for almost everything else.

So, Tuesday arrives, and off we pop to the bank to be greeted by a very pleasant young lady who invites us into the tiniest of offices.

She starts by taking our names and address and even though you'd think she'd know, asks us, "How can I help you today?"

"Well," I say, "we'd like to open up a joint Bank Account."

"That's great," she says, typing into her computer, confirming full names and ages and employment status etc. We then have a friendly little chat about how we came to be living in Ireland, and why, where we are, the usual stuff.

She then dumbfounds us by asking, "So, do you have a Utility Bill with your present address on it?"

I'm a little perplexed, I look at Ange, then continue, "Sorry, perhaps you misheard or misunderstood, we only moved here last … well not even a week till tomorrow, so obviously we don't have a utility bill for our address here: how could we? In fact," I continue, "I don't think we'll get any utility bills till we have an Irish bank account." I smile at her but it's far more in hope than expectation.

"I see," she says, tapping her Biro onto the desk. "That's a bit of a problem, I can't open a bank account without proof of address, that's why we need a utility bill." She's looking from one to the other of us.

"We've got this," Ange chirps up and delves into her handbag; she brings out the official lease document for the bungalow and hands it over to the young lady. "This should be proof of where we're living."

She scans it but says, "I'm afraid not, it needs to be an official bill." She seemed genuinely sorry that we're at a seemingly irresolvable impasse.

"Can I ask a question?"

"Please," she replies.

"If I sat here and told you I wanted to open a bank account, and deposit €150,000,000 in it, would you just sit there and say 'I'm sorry, not until you have a gas bill'?"

She smiled, which I must say was more than Ange did, shooting me daggers, and said, "I think if you had that much money you wouldn't be talking to me," and then, slightly more seriously, "You don't have that much money, do you?"

"Not yet," I replied.

There was then a somewhat lengthy silence that nobody wanted to end; fearing it would be more bad news, there was a bit of toe gazing and hand ringing. The young lady hammered at her keyboard, trying for a spark of enlightenment. Whether as a result of this hammering or not, I suspect not, she suddenly asked,

"Do you have any recent utility bills for you house in Doncaster?"

I looked at Ange. "Yes," she said. "In the box file in the car," and with that stood up and held her hand out for the car keys. "I'll only be two minutes," she says to the young lady as she's going out of the door.

While Ange is out, the young lady explains to me that there should be no problem whatsoever in opening an account for our Doncaster address. "You do still own the property, don't you?" I confirm this to be the case.

Ange returns and hands two or three relevant documents to the young lady, who starts to type, at the same time explaining to Ange what she has already told me.

After two or three minutes, the printer at the side of the desk starts to spew out page after page, in duplicate, of the necessary documents. Ange and I sign away on at least four pages; the young lady collates the signed pages, and hands us the unsigned copy.

She says, "I've put your present address down as a temporary one, so the cards etc will come there." I bring out our little bible of information, which is a small hardback notebook. I ask her to confirm our Bank Account number, Sort Code and IBAN Number which she does gladly.

She now stands, and shakes hands with both of us, saying, "That should be absolutely fine now; you'll get confirmation very quickly, and your cards will take no time to come through." She continued while showing us to the door, "Just leave it three or four weeks, and come in and change the permanent address on the account, to your present one, OK?"

We thanked her profusely for her time, patience, and, in the end, ingenuity. We left the bank feeling a little drained, but just a tad more Irish.

It wasn't lost on me that the reality of our situation was, now that we lived in Ireland; we had moved here TO LIVE; to obtain an Irish Bank account, we had to pretend we still lived in England.

Banks eh!

We stepped out of the bank into a sun-drenched Square, the hub of Roscommon. The Square is dominated by the stand-alone Bank of Ireland building, which forms an island with car parking that vehicles can completely circumnavigate. Originally built in the 1750s as a courthouse, it then became a Roman Catholic Church, and subsequently, its present use, as a bank. So, Justice, God, and Mammon have all been worshipped in this delightful cupola-topped building.

The building which houses Roscommon County Council Offices is somewhat less imposing, but is an impressive modern build, not far from the square.

Feeling on a roll in our search for Irishness, we decided to venture there now: as just as important as having an Irish bank account was the need for recognition by the state in the form of a PPSN card.

This is a Personal Public Service Number which is your fingerprint as far as Welfare, Tax, Education, and Health matters are concerned.

We didn't have to wait too long and were then interviewed separately in a little booth. Our interrogator was a delightful young lady, who had a great sense of humour. When asked if

I was comfortable, I replied, "Fine thank you, tea and biscuits?" She smiled and immediately pressed an imaginary button on her desk and said, "They're on the way!"

At the risk of sounding abstruse, this would become an extremely repetitive book if I told you that every time Irish people were friendly and nice, Irish people were friendly and nice.

This young lady was most definitely that. I couldn't help thinking about the few civil servants I'd had to encounter in England. Applying to replace a lost passport springs to mind. Never have I felt more intimidated by a civil servant, who had everything but a twin lightning bolt insignia on his shirt sleeve. Poor Ange, who also needed a replacement passport, was grilled even worse than I was; she of course had Irish parentage, which made her, as far as her interlocutor was concerned, one step up the ladder from untouchable.

This lass on the other hand was good fun. I kept looking up to the top of the glass divide that separated her world from mine; clamped there was a small black device that I could only think was a camera.

"Bit drastic," I said, looking up at the device. "What are you expecting me to do, all shut up as I am in this little cubicle?"

She laughed again. "All will be revealed," she replied and then I think wished she'd used a different phrase, as her cheeks slightly coloured.

The interview continued for a short time. No difficult questions, just background and a little life history. Finally, she looked up from her keyboard and screen and asked me to look at the camera. Her eyes stayed on the screen till finally she clicked a button and said, "That's great, thank you very much."

"I'll have a dozen," I replied as I got up to leave, I thanked her profusely and left, to let Ange enter.

Neither Ange nor I could remember for the life of us if we got our cards there and then, or if they arrived via the post some days later. Whichever it was, we were soon in possession of little lime green cards, with our fizzogs beautifully etched on, and our individual PPS numbers, ours and no one else's, just a little bit more Irish.

CHAPTER 3

THE ENGLISH PATIENT, AND THE DOCTOR

We had been in the bungalow no more than a couple of months when I developed an excruciating pain in my left knee. I could not for the life of me work out what the cause of this pain was. I had mown the lawn the previous day, completed the job in no discomfort whatsoever, yet suddenly I am in agony in any position other than sitting.

I managed to go to work for a couple of days, as driving was the easy bit, but no matter how well we strapped it up; how much Rub we applied; how many pain killers I took, nothing helped, the pain was dreadful. We even got a taxi into town so I could try J Arthur Guinness's internal remedy, and though that helped a little, it was no long-term cure, and agony getting to the loo and back.

I suffered two more dreadful nights, most of which were spent seated on the side of the bed, it was the only way I was pain free. Finally, I cracked, I could take no more. Using the yard brush as a crutch, I managed, at the crack of dawn, to drive to A&E in Roscommon, and hobble into outpatients, hoping that if nothing else, an X-Ray might throw some light on the matter.

The nice lady at reception asked me if I had a medical card, I explained I hadn't, but I still had a valid EEC Medical

Cover card that you needed for travel in Europe, and she was happy with that.

After a few minutes – this was still before 8.00 a.m. – a nurse came to collect me and, seeing the discomfort I was in just trying to stand, she fetched me a wheelchair. I was wheeled into the universally recognisable outpatient's area, then into a cubicle, and as she pulled the curtain about me asked if I could drop my trousers.

I had sat there for only a couple of minutes, keks round my ankles, when in comes this doctor, a big burly guy, and English. He's pleasant, makes small talk easily, sits immediately in front of me, and tries to lift my leg from the ankle. He notices me wince and places my foot back on the wheelchair footrest. "Rugby player?" he asks, as his healing hands are now gently working up my leg to the knee.

"Not for many years," I reply.

"Well, you won't be playing this weekend," he says with a smile. His fingers continue their investigation, pressing here, squeezing there.

After a few more minutes of what seems quite intense investigation he sits up. "I can tell you exactly what you've done here," he says. "You've ruptured your Plantaris muscle."

"My what?" says I, incredulously.

"Exactly," says he. "Nobody has ever heard of it but it's there." He draws a not very accurate finger up his own leg from ankle to knee. He carries on, "It's useless really, bit like your Appendix, but if you rupture either it hurts like a bugger." He went on, "I think it's about 13% of the population that aren't even born with one. These days, it's one of those bits that reconstructive surgeons use if they need a bit of ligament or tendon, or whatever." I may have misremembered exactly that last bit, but you get the drift. "Nothing we can do, no treatment just rest; that's all there is for it." He stood up to leave.

"Would it be possible to get some hospital-strength pain killers?" I plead, looking from one to the other. "And perhaps crutches?"

"I'm sure Sister can sort that out for you, can't you, Sister?"

"Yes doctor," she confirms, and both leave the cubicle, while I rehoist my trousers.

Sister returns with a shiny pair of aluminium crutches, and says she'll push me to my car. I must have looked like a loony being pushed across the hospital car park, holding a yard brush in front of me like some medieval lance. Once at the car, Sister opens the rear door and slides in the crutches, and brush that she's relieved me of, while I struggle into the driver's seat. At this point she leans in, and hands me a very small plastic bag with two, yes two, count them, two, white tablets. It looked just like the spare buttons you get with a new jacket or shirt. She says, "Whatever you do, don't take these till you get home, they're very strong." Well, I think to myself, let's hope each one lasts a week. I smile and thank her profusely for all the help she has been, which is considerable.

The kindness and compassion of nurses seems to be a global truth: what an unbelievable job these people do. It's a stain on Western civilisation that these people aren't remunerated nearly enough. It bugs me when you read of hospital administrators all earning tons more than the nursing staff.

I struggled back to report to Ange, guessing what a sympathetic reception I would receive. I hobbled in like a wounded soldier, returning from the front. Ange grunted something in a most sympathetic manner, turned over, and went back to sleep. Little Riley O Riley, our occasionally bellicose Jack Russell, was now occupying the warm patch I'd vacated, and had a most menacing look in its one, open eye that said, just you try it.

So, suitably placated by the familial love and affection I had received, I did a little more crutch practice, made a cup of tea, and using just the one crutch made it into the front room, sat down, and took half the tablets I'd been given. I went out like a light. Next thing I knew it was midday, and Ange was putting another cup of tea down on my chair-side table.

The doctor was right of course. It was slow progress; the pain gradually eased day by day, and I was crutchless after about eight days, but it was some time later before I was back trampolining!

CHAPTER 4

AVAST YE SWABS

Two or three weeks later, I was walking much better, but still needing to favour a slight limp. It came to our attention that there was to be a trip of some sort, or excursion out onto Lough Ree.

It was a beautiful summer's day, the lough looked at peace, waveless and windless. So, when we discovered that the local rescue boat, I think attached to the Sub-Aqua Club, was going to take people out onto the Lough, we quite fancied the idea. Who doesn't like messing about on the river? A light zephyr blowing through your hair, perhaps a gin and tonic. So, we two intrepid explorers presented ourselves at the appropriate time and place, to be given a life jacket. I'm thinking, life jacket? Why do I need a life jacket?

What was a little more perturbing, was they didn't have one that fitted me, at least not one I could fasten. Perhaps they think fat people are buoyant enough! When the guy in charge noticed that I couldn't fasten my jacket, he asked, "Can you swim?"

I nodded, "I can."

He came back with, "Ah you'll be fine if you can swim." At this point I'm having visions of being thrown in, so I'm the one they can practice rescuing. But then I think, no, they'd pick someone smaller than me to drag onto a boat. I smiled at Ange.

We walked down to the little quayside we have on the Lanesborough side of the river, and there, bobbing in the water, was a bright orange inflatable. Quite big I thought, and the engine at the back looked a monster, was this to be our pleasure craft?

No seats, it had NO seats.

We were helped to step down into the boat, then invited to sit on the rim of the inflatable, and weave our hand under, and grip onto, the inch-thick rope that was threaded through eyeholes, spaced around the rim of the craft. I didn't count how many of us landlubbers there were, but I'm guessing maybe twelve, or fourteen people, all seated in this way as we smoothly trundled out at a gentle pace into the Lough.

After only travelling a short distance, our captain, the only one who had a seat by the way, shouted above the hum of the engine, "Everyone holding on," and with that we gripped tighter, and he let her rip.

Not only was it earpoppingly noisy, but it was also breath-taking, because it was taking all my breath. The sheer power generated was palpable, it permeated your body like an electric current, and still faster we went.

I am more than happy to admit I was not a little scared. I was also not a little dry and getting wetter and wetter by the second. The craft would rise at the front, and such was the force of the boat as it hammered the water that we were constantly bombarded with plumes of spray. Everyone was getting drenched, and not only this, there was quite a puddle of water pooling visibly at the back of the craft where I was sitting. People were trying to lift and manoeuvre their feet in an attempt to keep them dry, but it was hopeless. The captain showed no sign of slowing down; he was in a one-boat, boat race that he was determined to win, if anything he was going quicker.

Before very long, we arrived at the point where, though exciting and fun at the start, with people giggling, and then screaming as though on a Fairground ride, it was now getting tedious, even annoying. The point had been made, if indeed there was a point to make. Ffs slow down.

There was an island ahead, an island probably nobody but the captain had ever seen before. It certainly wasn't visible from Lanesborough. As we got nearer to it, he did indeed start to slow down.

He actually stopped, letting the craft just bob about in the water. He then related some information about this island, but, quite frankly, I don't think anyone was in the slightest bit interested in the history lesson. Everyone just wanted to get back; we were all sodden. He turned the boat towards home and let it rip again.

I don't think he went quite as fast going back, it may be that we had just got used to it. I know that had I jumped overboard, and hung on to the rope, I could not have been any wetter. Nor could my rather good shoes, that were now sitting in at least five inches of water.

Eventually, we got back; the captain helped everyone step up onto the quay; we all thanked him as he did so, though I'm not sure how genuine all of these thanks were. Perhaps people were thanking him for getting us back alive. Quite frankly, I was more than a little peed off: the guy operating the boat must have known what was going to happen, and that 80% of us were inappropriately dressed, when he was handing out the life jackets.

We squelched our way back towards town, saturated, soaked, and somewhat sorrowful, and with each step water was coming up through the lace holes of my 'rather good shoes'.

I reached for my mobile, and although I had kept this in an inside pocket of my coat, under the life jacket that didn't fit, the leather case that protected the phone was, like everything else, dripping wet. I called our local, friendly taxi man, Tom.

Tom kindly collected us and took us home to change; thankfully he waited while we did so. We were soon heading back into town to enjoy a small and welcoming libation in the friendly Clarke's Bar.

As the afternoon wore on, the refreshment went down, I regaled the customers of our adventures like some piratical, salty old seadog. Stood at the bar, with one foot on the brass footrest, a flagon of ale in my right hand, conducting tales of adventurous, and lion-hearted derring do, about the day we fought the elements, the foamy brine, vicious imaginary Vikings, and the very monster itself. Indeed, how together, we tamed Lough Ree.

(Ange says I'm prone to exaggeration, but I can't think where she gets that idea from.)

CHAPTER 5

WATER, WATER EVERYWHERE

What of Lough Ree.

One of Ireland's best kept secrets: hardly anybody outside of Ireland has heard of it, we hadn't, and were Hibernophiles!

Well, it is the third largest lake in the republic; only Lough Corrib, which covers parts of Galway and Mayo ($176km^2$), and Lough Derg, also part of the Shannon waterway ($130km^2$), are larger.

Lough Ree comes in at a not-too-shabby $105km^2$. That's 41 sq. miles. How long is it? Well Jim O'Connor knows, because in 2012 he swam its entire length for charity, a mere 33.91km, or if you prefer 21.07miles. It *only* took him 13 hours and 34 minutes. What a fantastic achievement that was. At its widest point, Lough Ree is seven miles across and that makes it a substantial piece of water in anybody's estimation.

Lanesborough/Ballylegue is the first crossing point at the north end of the Lough, where it effectively becomes the River Shannon again, at the southern end this honour goes to the town of Athlone. As well as the aforementioned boundary between Counties Longford and Roscommon, and the provincial boundary between Leinster and Connaught, the Leinster county of Westmeath has a county border with Longford in the lower south eastern section of the Lough.

The shape of the Lough is indescribable, other than to say when looking at it on a map it resembles a Rorschach Ink Blot. If you were able to walk around Lough Ree it would be a gentle trek of some 191 kilometres.

Unfortunately, as with so many of the midland Loughs, you can't walk around Lough Ree. This is because there are not many access points. With the Midland Loughs being situated in the predominantly bog-land area of the country, they tend not to have hard shorelines, but marshy boggy ones. Even with a Lough, which, let's face it, is the enormous size of Lough Ree, there are actually very few spots you can view it. Wherever there is a hard shoreline, then tiny communities and small jetties, and perhaps the odd Marina, have been built, but it really is quite a hidden and secluded piece of water, certainly at the northern half. There is a little more activity when you get down towards Athlone.

This is perhaps why the aforementioned Monster is so rarely spotted. Loch Ness, pah!

The most famous sighting came on May 28th 1960, when three priests out fishing saw a large black animal swimming up the Lough. Now these men were pious, stalwart men of the cloth, so it would be preposterous to suggest anything like drink was involved here. Sure enough, they witnessed a creature rise and fall below the Lough in the shape of a loop. They estimated it to be about six feet in length, so, it's not Godzilla then, but nevertheless, considerably bigger than anything else that should be in there. This sighting made the national press and was even picked up by the BBC at the time. There's many a pleasure-craft that has traversed Lough Ree and reported a bump against the hull where there should have been nothing but water.

Be afraid, be (just a little bit) afraid.

Another thing that Lough Ree has, apart from monsters, is fish and it has a lot of big nasty, pointy-toothed ones, called Pike, or Northern Pike, to be more accurate. The town hosts the Lough Ree Pike Classic. This is serious fishing and has a prize fund of €10,000 and fishermen arrive from all over to try and bag one of these beauties. In one such event, only two or three years ago, 17 Pike were caught that measured over one metre in length, and the €3000 prize for the longest was won by a tiddler that came in at 108.5cms, that is an astounding 3'6" in old money. I don't know how much this fish weighed, but they regularly come in at over 30lbs.

They can live to be well into their twenties, and though in some countries they are considered quite a delicacy, here, so I am told, most are thrown back because they are very, very, bony and quite difficult to eat. I am also told that it's not that unusual, when opening one of these creatures up, to perhaps find a dead rodent being digested away inside. That sort of puts me off gutting one and throwing it into the pan to enjoy with a few chips.

There are a number of islands dotted about Lough Ree, many of which at one time or another were inhabited, and many others have archaeological remains of fortifications. Some are still farmed but these days the farmers are mainland based. One of these islands which is found towards the northern, or our end of the Lough, is Inishcleraun; it is believed that this island was first inhabited in 540 AD by Saint Diarmuid, who was a teacher of Saint Ciaran of Clonmacnoise.

Clonmacnoise, is a most wonderfully preserved ancient monastic site, and settlement on the River Shannon just below Athlone. It should most definitely be on the bucket list of any visitor to Ireland who is even remotely interested in the ancient history of the place. It has one of the best interactive visitor centres we have been to, and it really is very impressive. (Have a look at heritageireland.ie)

Inishcleraun was a place of learning and pilgrimage for centuries, and contains the ruins of six churches, graveyards, and a fort for protection against Viking raids.

One of Inishcleraun's most famous residents was Queen Medbh (pronounced Maeve).

The Irish language is an amazingly difficult thing to get one's head round and I have absolutely no intention of trying to do so. The above island that I am talking about would be, I understand, Inis Cloithreann in the vernacular as it were, this can be Anglicised to be Inchcleraun, yet the form I've used is a mixture of the two which seems to be equally acceptable.

The founding fathers of this republic were absolutely right to give great credence to, and rejoice in, their own Gaelic language, but it's a bastard.

Back to Medbh, who was some girl I tell you. If half of the folklore written about her is true, then she makes Lucretia Borgia look like Mother Teresa. She was the Queen of Connaught, had many husbands and numerous lovers, and didn't bat an eyelid at murdering people.

Formally married to the King of Ulster, she is perhaps

most famous for instigating The Cattle Raid of Cooley. This was a plan to steal the King of Ulster's prize Bull, Donn Cúailnge. She had initially offered wealth, land, and sexual favours, for a loan of this great stud bull, and initially her offer was to be accepted, but, due to a breakdown in communications – it is said that the messenger who was to deliver this offer got drunk, probably stopped in Clarkes's on the way – a message along the lines of 'if you don't accede, we'll take it by force anyway' was delivered. At which point the original acceptance was declined. This resulted in vast armies being raised, with battles and skirmishes all over, and there was immense bloodshed on both sides, imagine, there are people who think Game of Thrones is fiction. Not a bit of it!

Anyway, after all this blood-letting and debauchery, Queen Medbh made it to a relatively old age, so she put her bloody sword, and licentious libido behind her, and retired to the island of Inishcleraun on Lough Ree, to keep chickens and grow vegetables.

Here she took to bathing regularly in a little pool. However, it didn't end well. One of the many people that Medbh was allegedly responsible for the death of was her own sister Clothra. Now, Clothra's son, named Furbaide, who it is said was delivered by Caesarean after Clothra's murder, was a bit hacked off about not only losing, but never actually meeting his mum, so swore revenge on wicked Aunty Medbh.

So he judged the distance from the shore to the small pool where Medbh bathed most days. It is said he practiced and practiced with his sling, until he unfailingly hit the correct length, time after time.

The next time he saw Medbh bathing, he unerringly took

aim and whoosh … she was dead, killed with a bit of hard cheese. This last bit was said to be invented by later tellers of this tale, in an attempt to dishonour Medbh, but I'm inclined to think it's where the saying comes from, that means 'tough luck'.

It is also why, more importantly, our own local Lanesborough Distillery produces Sling Shot Gin, and jolly good it is too.

A forerunner to the more recent GAA football results occurred in the year 937. A team of Limerick Vikings travelled up to Lough Ree for a punch-up with a team of Dublin Vikings and, as has now become the norm, the Dubs won …

(You will have gathered that I'm no historian, and the above has been gleaned from the odd book and the internet. With that in mind, I am totally responsible for any inaccuracies, fantasies, flaws, or falsehoods there might be in the above tale. A friend once explained to me that the Irish never let the truth get in the way of a good story.)

CHAPTER 6

NÍ NEART GO CUR LE CHÉILE
NO STRENGTH WITHOUT COMMUNITY

We hadn't lived in Lanesborough very long, when we became aware of a major forthcoming event, and one of particular interest to Ange. Our local newspaper, The Longford Leader, carried an appeal for stewards to help marshal the upcoming Two Provinces Triathlon.

Neither of us had ever taken part in such a thing. Well, it goes without saying I hadn't, but Angie was an accomplished runner in her day, having completed several marathons in very good times indeed, so at least the running appealed to her. Off she went to volunteer her assistance.

When Ange did the London marathon, she did not have a recorded time to give the organisers, so was forced to join in with the masses at the back. She had previously completed a marathon before the London, and did quite well. On the day of the London event, the starting clock had 16 minutes on it when Ange got to the gate, so considering her finishing time was three hours and a few seconds, she did pretty damn well. It's a good job I didn't meet her for a few years after this, because I'd have never caught her in those days!

When the day arrived, the size of the event soon became apparent: as we gathered in the village hall for Ange to be allocated her station, and receive instructions, there were dozens of volunteers all milling round waiting for the same.

Ange was allocated an area of road towards the end of the running race, which was the third discipline; so, we had a little time to wander down to the Lough to watch the first event, which was the swimming.

I, of course, would probably have made a first-class triathlete were it not for the fact that I was never much of a runner, none-too-fussed about cycling, and only ever liked to swim with naked women and dogs. As yet, I have only managed the second part of the latter, but I live in hope.

The whole area was buzzing, 600 or more competitors effected quite a logistics headache, and the need for so many stewards and marshals became quickly apparent. The chief organiser, on the loud hailer, was most efficient; like an Italian traffic-cop marshalling and pointing the various groups of multi-coloured swim caps into their own sections; slowly, as though someone had emptied a tube of Smarties, he directed all the red there and the blue there and the green over there. Pockets of the different levels and groups of swimmers emerged.

There were also competitors who were only doing what is termed as Aqua-Bike, ie: no running; there were others doing a much smaller version, in an event called Try-a-Tri; there was even a Kiddie-Thon. It was a brilliantly organised event, and much of the community, if not taking part or helping out, were on the sidelines cheering the participants on.

What there wasn't, was a great splashing start, because each wave of swimmers started from in the water. This disappointed a little: I thought the idea of everyone running and diving in much more exciting; sadly, not practical or safe. That said, the sight of the first wave of maybe 50 or so people, all setting out at once, was still some spectacle. And, what a long way to go; 300 metres to the first buoy; round that, 150 metres to the next; round that, then 300 metres home. 750 meters is a fair old swim; particularly to someone like me who thinks a width of the local pool an achievement worthy of certification.

Then, the good buggers, having finally made it back to terra firma, do this tarantella-resembling dance, trying to remove wet-suits whilst running towards the cycle park, at the same time as trying to put cycling shoes on their feet; then cycle 20km. That's a long way in a car!

And as if that wasn't enough, when they get back from their cycle-ride, they go and run 5km through our glorious woods and local roads.

If you didn't know how long a 750-metre swim, a 20km cycle ride, and a 5km run might take, just have a little think and try and guess. No!

I'll tell you then, the winner did all three in less than an hour. Staggering!

The whole experience was a wonderful example of how this community we were already learning to love came together. I heard nobody moan about roads being shut, or the extra traffic, or the children's play-area being overrun with competitors. Nobody was complaining about anything; everybody just getting stuck in to make the event the really fantastic success it was.

Many of the locals, not involved in any way, lined the streets, cheering and clapping. Their enthusiasm urging the competitors on.

It was a joyous episode, and it made me think we'd come to live in not too bad a place.

So, this being a Saturday, we went to the pub to talk about it.

The most obvious example of Community here in Ireland is the Tidy Towns organisation which promotes real pride in the places people live. There are over 900 Tidy Towns groups throughout Ireland and the work they do is fantastic. We have such a group for both sides of the river here, and, without them, the town would not look as clean and tidy, or as well decorated at Christmas, as it does.

A real effort is made by the TT groups; they pretty up the streets with flower barrels and hanging baskets. The odd area that might have been scrub is cultivated into flower beds. On the Ballyleague side, a number of seats and benches have been made to rest the weary walker. Only recently, a new bench has been situated at the top of the road, leading down to the Marina in Ballyleague. The back of this bench is a rather beautiful sculpture of two men in a rowing position. These are said to represent St Brendan the Navigator, and his brother St Fáithleach, who it is said visited this area by boat *circa* 520AD, so, just the 1500th anniversary of that then.

Another example of the community coming together here are the Mens Sheds. An idea which originated in Australia, but has become very popular in Ireland, where there are now over 450 such groups. We have a Mens Shed on each side of the river.

More often than not, though not exclusively, they have members with skills that can benefit the community:

woodworking/gardening. What they always have is a kettle, and they can, for some people, be a real antidote to loneliness.

I have attached myself to the Lanesborough group. We concentrate more on Social History in so much as there is a fortnightly social-gathering and, every six or eight weeks or so, a trip out to an historical attraction. Just before I allied myself to the group, they had enjoyed trips to the Titanic Centre in Belfast, and to Croke Park in Dublin. Since I tagged along, and before Covid put an end to such pleasantries, I have enjoyed trips to Glasnevin, Dublin Zoo, Leinster House, (The Parliament), and the Irish Whiskey Museum.

A good breakfast on the way out, a good dinner on the way home, and good company all day. What more could you ask for?

CHAPTER 7

WITH A HEY DIDDLE DIDDLE

One common denominator to at least three of the four pubs we have is that they have, respectively, on Saturday, Sunday and Wednesday evenings, traditional Irish music.

The Saturday sessions are often played by a more established group, whereas the other two sessions consist of local talent brought together for what can best be described as a Jam session.

This happens all over Ireland, and it is a quite remarkable cultural experience. One time, while on holiday in Connemara (a beautiful mountainous area on the west coast of Ireland), we were sat in a pub, enjoying a couple of jars of what does you good after a lovely day's sightseeing. We only had Jess then, and she was curled up under the table, when a young lady walked in with a violin, followed soon after by a guy with an acoustic guitar. A chap who had been standing at the bar, turned, and sat with the other two and took out of his inside-jacket-pocket a tin whistle. Next, a quite elderly gentleman with a small accordion-type instrument, not sure what it's called, came in and sat down with them next.

The bar was now getting crowded when this young chap comes in, carrying way above his head a large box. He proceeded to join the others, and positioned the box, which I could now see was a T Chest that had been cut in half, in such a way as to be part of the ensemble. He sat on the box and, leaning forward, playing it with both hands between his legs; this had become the band's percussion instrument.

I love the way these sessions evolve; any of the musicians might start up a tune they know, and the others just step in and join them when they've got hold of the tune or rhythm of the piece. This was one of those evenings, not uncommon in Ireland, where "We'll just have one more" turned into a stay of an extra couple of hours, so good was the entertainment, and of course, the Guinness.

From long before coming to Ireland, Ange and I were established early doors drinkers, we were rarely out much past 6.30 p.m. There were of course the odd exceptions, usually when we had visitors, or some other event had shifted our routine. One such time was a Sunday evening. Ange had been away all day in purgatory (St. Patrick's on Lough Derg)! I said I'd meet her at Clarke's at about 9.30 which was when she was due back. As I was walking up the road the coach was just pulling up. I met her off it and explained in no uncertain terms that I was the one in purgatory, waiting till 9.30 p.m. on a Sunday to get a beer. Just as we were entering Clarke's we could hear loud music coming from just up the road in the Swan Tavern. We had a drink, but Clarke's seemed unusually quiet, and we wondered if everyone was up the road. So, we finished our beers and went to check it out. As we walked into what was indeed an absolutely rammed pub, and fought our way to the bar, the band struck up a delightful little ditty to the tune of 'My Old Man's a Dustman', however the words had been changed to: 'My Old Man's a Provo'.

*

Well, my old man's a Provo with a beret and gun
I haven't seen him lately he's always on the run
He looks so really trendy in his shades and DM boots
Far cooler than those other dads with ties and shirts and suits...

The Brits and Police harass me, each time that I go out,
They ask me if I seen me da or if he's been about,
I say 'Mind yer own business, now just leave me alone,
You shower are only jealous, you've no fathers of your own'.

*

There are a few more verses but never did I feel so English!

By the way, it wasn't the context of the songs that has prevented us venturing out more on a weekend evening, it's just that no one in Ireland seems to have a watch, or feel the need for sleep. Everything happens so late; never do these evenings start on time, and they rarely seem to stop.

I have participated in two local quiz nights in the last twelve months or so. Quiz nights are still a very popular fundraising activity here: anyway, both were supposed to start at 9.00 p.m., but on each occasion a question wasn't asked before 10.20 p.m.

On the odd occasion, we have ventured to a Wednesday session, traditional music from 10.00 p.m. As though this wasn't late enough to start anything, except your Cocoa, you'll be lucky to hear a note played before 10.45 p.m.

But when it does start it's fantastic, we love it, and in time when retirement comes, we'll go more often, but at the moment I'm still working and late-night music is not a companionable bedfellow with early morning starts.

The make-up of these sessions can vary, but often there might be two Guitars, a Fiddle or two, a Banjo, a Snare Drum, Uilleann Pipes, Tin Whistle, a Bodhran and even more brilliant to my mind, the human voice.

The Irish have this delightful and wonderfully uncomplicated attitude to singing. It doesn't matter if you are not pitch perfect; how would I know anyway. There's a complete lack of embarrassment or nerves; it seems as natural as talking. Men, women, young or old, people just get lost in the moment. Having been to both Wednesday and Sunday sessions, it's easy to think that it will be the same people playing, not a bit of it. I'm staggered at just how many different people have a musical talent in such a small community, and this of course is replicated throughout every townland, hamlet, village, and town in the country. It's a most wonderful cultural resource for the Irish nation to have.

One other thing that happens quite regularly at these events, something else that the Irish seem to have a wonderful penchant for, is poetry. Often, though by no means always, someone will stand and recite from memory, some poem, or maybe even a humorous short tale, listened to with great deference by all present; it's just another aspect of the wonderful enlightenment here.

CHAPTER 8

OK SO IT'S NOT AN ALP

On one of my first visits into our local newsagents we were having a discussion, when the term 'mountain' was used. This made me smile. "No, no," I was told. "We all know it as the mountain." What Joe was referring to was Slieve Bawn, or Sliabh Ban or Sliabh Baghna, whichever way we spell it, and we'll use the first one, Slieve Bawn (phonetically, Shleeve Born) is a hill; yes, it is, it's not a mountain. As I understand it, one of the accepted qualifications for a hill to become a mountain is that it rises to over 2000 feet. Slieve Bawn does no such thing. At its highest point it is 860 feet. This is a hill, though from now on it's the 'Mountain'.

What it is, is beautiful, a really elegant tree-covered monolithic rock which rises Ulhuru-like out of the flat boglands of Roscommon and Longford. It's perhaps not quite as dramatic as Ulhuru, but I hope this paints a picture.

If you travel north-east from Ballyleague towards Strokestown, the 'Mountain' dominates your journey to the left, though what really catches the eye are the twenty, giant wind turbines that comprise the Slieve Bawn Windfarm. Some people hate these structures, and think they are a real blot on the landscape, but I can't help thinking that it's a better idea than industrially ripping the Bog to pieces to feed power stations and the like. (This activity has now ceased.) You never know, someday we might invent an even better method of supplying our energy, at which point these turbines can be taken down ... we most definitely can't put the Bog back.

A number of tiny communities and smallholdings are dotted about its slopes and base. Small, whitewashed farmsteads in the fields and up the lanes; large bungalows hug the Strokestown road through Cloontuskert, and Curraghroe; ancient places in many respects. There was an Abbey at Cloontuskert, though now only a wall, serving as the perimeter to the graveyard remains.

The mountain itself is now a designated recreation area, numerous trails and tracks are available to the walker and the mountain-biker.

A car park has been fashioned halfway up the mountain on the Roscommon side. From this car park you have alternative ways to get up on to the top of the mountain. Very, very steep steps have been cut through the woods, or you can follow the engineer's road which takes a more meandering, but gentle route up, passing close to the jumbo turbines. The sheer size and whoosh of which is quite awesome. This will eventually deposit you towards the top; at this point a number of trails are available.

We take the trail signposted 'Holy Year Cross'. This is a large concrete structure that was erected by local people for the Christian Jubilee of 1950. It was from this Cross that we first set eyes on some of the islands of Lough Ree.

If you are blessed with a good day weather-wise, and I don't see the point of doing it if you're not, what's the point of climbing Everest if it's going to be cloudy on top? Then you will be treated to stunning views over County Roscommon to the west and County Longford to the east. The first thing you realise and appreciate more is that the Mountain is a real oasis of height in the flat midlands. It's some distance to where you can see the faint outline of other hills.

What you are also looking at, particularly when looking east, is the Bog land of this region.

I can think of no better description of, or tribute to, Slieve Bawn, than a selected few stanzas of this wonderful poem, written by local resident Jimmy Brehon.

SLIEVE BAWN

When in childhood I viewed my surroundings
I used to think the old hill reached the sky
And that one day I'd climb up to heaven
And save myself having to die.

And I dreamed that Slieve Bawn was the Mountain
On which Noah's Ark went aground
And the bulk of that famous vessel
It was waiting up there to be found.

Then at last when my wings had grown stronger
Came the day of my childhood's big thrill
When achieving my greatest ambition
I stood proudly on top of the hill.

The old Ark of my dream it was missing
With no trace of its cargo or crew
Still, I found heaven there all about me
Where in patches the brown heather grew.

A lark was ecstatically singing
High up in a summer blue sky
Startled Grouse fluttered up from the heather
And a Hare stole from cover nearby.

In their yellow and pink coloured blossoms
The whin bushes were dressed up to kill
The whole scene on the day of that outing
Is engraved on my memory still.

Maybe someday some statesman or monarch
The greatest the world has seen
Will discover his roots on the Mountain
Then we'll have our own Ballyporeen.[2]

And in fancy I see not the Mountain
Being preserved as a national park
And I see the whin blossoms returning
With the heather, the grouse, and the lark.

But more often I see other pictures
Flash onto my own mental screen
Haunting pictures of faces and places
That were part of the days that have been.

---

[2] *Ancestral home of Ronald Reagan.*

But there's one that I want to keep with me
'Till my last breath of life has been drawn
'Tis the masterpiece by Mother Nature
The enchanting old hill of Slieve Bawn.

Jimmy Brehon, Doughill, Curraghroe …

(Reproduced by kind permission from relatives.)

CHAPTER 9

"HOLMES, I'M IN THE BOG"

There is still something special about a peat fire. One of our abiding memories is an almost Christmas Card scene of taking the dogs for a mid-morning walk, all wrapped up on a crisp frosty Christmas day in Lismore, County Waterford. As we walked down to the beautiful Blackwater River, the still air was full of the sweet fragrance of peat burning, and many of the houses we walked past, or could see, had plumes of fragrant blue-grey smoke rising vertically into the icy air.

In Ireland the bog represents something absolutely fundamental, it's a way of life, a source of both income and energy. And there is a lot of it, or was ....

In 1933, Ireland was a very young independent country of only 11 years, but it realised the importance of turf to the country's economic development, and so set up the Turf Development Board, this later, in 1946, became Bord na Mona, which still operates today.

Peat was dug on an industrial scale and power stations were built to convert this great natural and national resource into much needed electricity. Bord na Mona had its own power station at Edenderry, but also supplied the power stations of the ESB (Electricity Supply Board) one of which, The Lough Ree Power Station, is situated in Lanesborough.

But things have now changed.

For reasons political, economic, and ecological, it has been decided by the powers that be that the bogland areas of Ireland are no longer a justifiable resource when it comes to industrial power generation.

The Bog has now come to the end of its life as an industrial resource and has been discontinued as a material for use in power stations, hence the Wind Farm on Slieve Bawn and many, many others like it across Ireland. One future advantage of this decision is that many miles of the miniature railway lines (used to transport the peat to the power station) that criss-cross the bog may well be turned into paths for walking and cycling; by their very nature the bog lands are very interesting habitats for both flora and fauna, with a rewarding diversity of each.

The Royal Canal also crosses the area and will tie up well in creating a real network for the more athletic holidaymaker, we hope so anyway. Wind Farms are everywhere now in Ireland and there are, as I write, plans to build many more on the now industrially defunct areas of bogland around Lanesborough and the surrounding district.

However, to drive past fields where turf has been cut for domestic use, and to see the carefully accumulated piles of material laid out to dry in neat columns, is to bear witness to centuries of continuity in the life of the Irish people, to which many retain a strong attachment.

CHAPTER 10

WORK, WORK, WORK

We're settling into our new home, and while we are loving the area, and the people we meet, we are none too happy with the bungalow we are renting. As much as anything, this comes from the frustration at not being able to do anything with it; put our own fingerprint down. It frustrates the hell out of Ange, who unfortunately is spending most of her days in it. She is happy to walk, mile after mile, with the dogs, but the walk always ends with having to go back to the bungalow.

We need a plan.

I'm not sure how or from whom the idea came about, but suddenly she was scouring the websites for Mystery Shopping opportunities. This was something neither of us had done before, and an area of expertise neither of us had, but everybody has to start somewhere.

The beauty of this plan was that I was travelling to all compass points of this beautiful land, and this enabled Ange to pick and apply for jobs that coincided with my journey plan. It meant being a little more organised than I usually was, but I started to plan three weeks in front, which meant Ange could apply for jobs on that route, and, if there weren't any, well, life wasn't so bad now if she did have to stay at home the odd day.

Suddenly the prospect of this work refocused both our outlooks. Ange came with me most days, unless I was local, and the jobs she was taking on took us to many places we might never had visited otherwise; in fact, we were getting to know the country very well. At this point in time, we were still unsure whether or not we were going to stay in this area or look elsewhere for a permanent home, and this gave us a great opportunity to look around.

The work is certainly different from anything either of us had done before. I say either of us because it soon became apparent that one of the key customer groups to these Market Research companies are car brands. This would entail visiting a showroom and being very interested in purchasing a new car, often a specific model, which was all part of the feedback the manufacturer wanted. These visits would often entail taking a test drive. Ange wasn't overly keen on this idea, though she is a perfectly able driver, but the money is good, so I was the one who tended to do these. We have also both done a number of financial institutions and have regularly enquired about investing considerable sums of money. I wish!

One of Ange's regular engagements is at one of the continental supermarkets that are now everywhere, you know the ones, they're nearly an anagram, geddit? She does the five nearest to where we live, every month, and it's a nice little earner. Sometimes, the reports you have to fill in can be a little exhausting, and you often find yourself repeating answers. I paraphrase the sort of things you are asked at the very start of this book.

I've often departed the car showrooms feeling that it's all a bit of a burlesque. I'll give you an example.

I'll tell you about a showroom I did, I won't say where for obvious reasons.

The instructions from the manufacturer that the salesman should follow are very specific. They must demonstrate all the car's external features, starting at the rear driver's side, walking in a clockwise direction, finishing at the driver's door, where they should invite you to sit in. If the car they are exhibiting is inside the showroom, they should point out the features and benefits of the drive specification, and then ask you to take a Test Drive, on which they should accompany you.

On the test drive, they should re-emphasise the quality of the drive, and point out again some of the features and benefits of the vehicle and dashboard area

Back in the showroom, depending whether my instructions are to act as a cash buyer or a trade in, it's nearly always a trade in, the salesman should offer me a drink while he assesses my own vehicle. After he has made this assessment, he returns, and starts punching at his computer. Normally he will print off a quote and go through it with you.

This is the first time you know what he's offering for your car, and how much the purchase will cost you. If you are wanting to finance all or part of it, another sheaf of papers might appear, offering variable costs over say, 36, 48, or 60 months.

Most people have bought a car at some point and have a fairly good idea how it all works.

This is what happened on this particular visit.

I walk into the showroom and approach a salesman sat behind a desk.

He looks up, "Can I help you?"

"I hope so," I say, "I'm interested in a ***** ******"

The salesman picks up a bunch of keys off his desk and THROWS them to me, "There's one just outside the door," he says. "Take it for a spin; come back and tell me what you think. If you don't bring it back, I'll know you're having it." He laughs at this, though I guess he's said it a thousand times before.

So, I do as he asks; I take the car for a drive. 15 minutes around town, on my own, and return to the showroom.

When I get back, he invites me to sit. "Like it?" he asks. "Trade in?" he commands.

"Yes," I say. "Mine's the white Yeti," pointing to the car park.

"Would you like a tea or coffee; its absolute crap," he adds, "but you can have one if you want."

"I'm fine thanks," I say.

And with that I hand him my keys, and off he goes to look round my car.

He returns after an improbably short time, asks for my details, and starts banging away at the computer; he looks up at me over his glasses. "Finance?" he says, "48 months?" I need to get a finance quote as part of the job. "Yeah that's fine," I reply.

In no time at all, the printer at the side of his desk is spewing paper.

He picks a sheet up and, pointing with a pen, says, "That's the Trade Price; that's the very generous discount I've given you because I'm feeling good today." He then whispers, "That's what I've allowed against your car; it's a bit too generous, but hey!" At this point he actually winks at me; you couldn't make it up. "So that's the bottom line and it doesn't get any better than that; that's the best price I can do."

Part of my remit is to ask if that's the very best price, so I study the sheet he's handed me as forensically as I can. After a few moments I say, "This is definitely the very best price you can offer?"

"Can't do a cent less," he says. "Would if I could," and thrusts his hand out, expecting me to shake it and close the deal.

I decline and say, "It looks good, but I've learned not to spend this much money without first discussing it with the wife."

"No problem," he says, standing up and offering his hand again. This time I take it and he says, "I'll give you a ring tomorrow, and we can tie it all up by weekend," and with that the appointment is over.

The point in my relating this story is that this salesman did absolutely nothing from the 'How to sell a *****' manual but his corner of the showroom was wallpapered with 'Salesman of the Month' awards. There were dozens of them; two 'Salesman of the Year' awards were on his desk; there was just no space for any more awards. He probably had drawers full.

I would love to see the marketing guy from ***** who wrote the manual (probably never actually sold a car in his life) watch this guy at work!

No matter how poor a score this salesman achieved when my report was handed to *****, I suspect the Dealership Principal, when he received said report, would be laughing it straight into the wastepaper bin.

It reminds me of that classic old cartoon of the frustrated customer, banging one fist on the counter and pointing with the other hand, and the guy behind the computer screen nonchalantly saying, "It's no good pointing at it, sir, the computer says we haven't got one."

Very few of the Market Research jobs that come our way can we do together, so we were delighted to be asked if we would like to take part in the awards scheme for the Irish Restaurants Association. Would we!

We received through the post a number of vouchers bearing the august organisation's logo, which we were to pass onto the clients as payment at the end of the particular assignment we were doing. In the case of fine dining, I had to make a recorded reservation call, and then go and enjoy some good, no, exceptional nosebag. Not all our visits were fine dining though, perhaps eight, as other categories might include Cafés, Pubs, best children's food etc, it's a hard job but somebody has to do it.

We enjoyed some delicious meals in many of the best restaurants and hotels in Counties Longford and Roscommon, almost all were first class. I would love to relate some tales of disastrous under-cooked or burnt food, but sadly no, there really is a very high standard of dining here. That there seem so many restaurants, I think ties in with the lack of availability of food in the majority of pubs, only in the main tourist areas, in our region places like Carrick on Shannon do you find much pub food.

Towards the end of our first year of restaurant awards, we got a call asking if we would like to go to Blacklion.

There are a lot of people in Ireland who would know

immediately what was being asked of us. Blacklion is a very small village in County Cavan, right on the border with the north, and is the home of Neven Maguire's restaurant, MacNean House.

In Ireland, Neven Maguire is one of the best-known TV chefs. He makes a lot of cookery programmes, most that highlight the superb quality of the Irish produce he insists on using. He also comes across as an exceptionally nice bloke and has authored many cookbooks.

For many people who like to fine dine, to eat at Blacklion would without doubt be a bucket list tick, however, for normally financed folk like us, this becomes a once in a lifetime opportunity.

Here's the rub; we were to do the visit on a Thursday evening, I had made the booking some three weeks earlier, and this was the first gap they had; if we had wanted to visit on a weekend the wait would have been considerably longer.

Come the Tuesday prior to our visit, I get hit with very serious tummy trouble; without going into too much detail, I had to visit the doctor for some Plutonium Grade Imodium. Thank God I didn't have a cough.

I spent the rest of that Tuesday and all day Wednesday just sitting in front of the telly, having an occasional sip of water, making the odd dash, and nothing else. Thursday arrived, and to be honest I still didn't feel too great, though mercifully the evacuations had ceased, perhaps the tablets were kicking in at last.

We put our posh togs on, and off we set for the first evening course at 7.30. I was praying that I was going to be OK, I really wanted to enjoy the experience and I think the headline 'Diner cacks pants at table seven' would have done nothing for Neven's reputation. Thankfully, that didn't happen; what did happen was this...

The building was very plush, and, on entering, we were shown into a very pleasant bar area where we had a drink and mingled for a few minutes. After not very long, and bang on time, we were shown through to our table. We were immediately struck by how young the waitresses and waiters were, though this did not for one second diminish their excellence. One of these young people delivered to our table a shallow square wooden box draped in a piece of spotless starched linen which contained a number of pieces of bread in various shapes and designs. The waitress very carefully explained to us the type of each piece of bread; sourdough, soda, made with Guinness etc., etc. and confirmed that all the breads were made in the restaurant, fresh that day.

At this point I noticed that the box that the bread was in was quite heavy, I soon realised that this was because, under the cloth on which the bread sat, the box was full of heated ceramic baking beans.

We were then visited by the Sommelier, who, to be frank, didn't look old enough to drink, let alone to have an encyclopedic knowledge of the grape and all its diverse manifestations. But she was terrific and, she was a she, which surprised me, I'm not sure why it should, but it did.

The menu consisted of a starter, then three other courses in which we had a choice from two or three dishes, and finally a choice of two sweets.

To put it simply, we ate the best food either of us had ever tasted; I'll tell you what I had:

Sweetcorn Velouté

Ham Hock with Celeriac Remoulade and Apple.

Hake with a Nut Crust and Sun-dried Tomato Fregola.

Fillet of Dry Aged Beef with Smoked Celeriac and Mushroom á la Crème.

Chocolate Fondant, with Tiramisu, Cappuccino Semifreddo and Coffee Ice Cream.

Ange, who is vegetarian, had:

Sweetcorn Velouté

Goat's Cheese Fritters with Goat's Cheese Pâté and Hazelnut Vinaigrette.

Wild Mushroom Pithivier with Pickled Mushrooms and Black Garlic.

Ricotta and Chard Ravioli with Toasted Pine Nuts and Smoked Garlic Velouté.

Rhubarb Cheesecake with Ginger and Rhubarb Parfait and Poached Rhubarb.

I won't say what this cost, or would have done, if we were paying, other than to say, if I was out drinking in Blacklion on a Friday night, I wouldn't be saying to the lads "Let's pop into Nev's for a take-away on the way home". The whole experience was something neither of us had encountered in our lives. The service was *par excellence*. If you went to the loo, fortunately I didn't have to, phew! when you got back your napkin had been refolded and was as immaculate as when you first sat down. Absolutely EVERYTHING about the whole evening was extraordinary. We may never do this again (unless those numbers come up) but I would recommend anybody who likes this kind of thing to make a beeline to Blacklion; you will not be disappointed. But book early, I found this from the Irish Times in 2008 – "The recession must be biting" a fellow diner said to me as we sat down to dine in MacNean House and Restaurant in Blacklion, Co Cavan. "Neven's waiting list is down to six months."

CHAPTER 11

TOP GEAR

I used to spend hours and hours on some of the busiest roads in England. The M62 and the M1 are nobody's idea of fun; I have spent over six hours queuing behind a dreadful accident on the M62, on two occasions.

These roads are busy at the quietest of times, but at rush hour they are a nightmare. I used to travel a lot to the other side (western) of Manchester, but if I hadn't got to the other side by 7.00 a.m., woe betide me. It did mean, however, that I developed an encyclopaedic knowledge of where all the good breakfasts on Merseyside were, because at all times I preferred to sit with Tea, Toast, and the Telegraph, to the option of Traffic.

In Ireland, as you might expect, Dublin has a rush hour, with lesser versions in some of the other larger towns, but we definitely benefit from economies of scale here. Where I live now, avoiding rush hour means having a good knowledge of local milking times; all you are going to get stuck behind here is a heard of full-uddered Friesians, or the odd crawling tractor, and more often than not the morning after you've had the car washed.

In comparison to the first few pages of this book, the roads in Ireland are now first class. There is a motorway system of over 900km; almost all of these fan out from the M50 which is the semi-circular motorway that envelopes Dublin. Wherever you travel in Ireland, it won't be long before you come across new roads being built, or existing ones being upgraded. From our central location we can be almost anywhere north or south in three and a half hours, journeys that not many years ago would have taken the best part of a day.

In Ireland they have VRT. Let me explain, new cars are more expensive here than they are in the UK; considerably so. Vehicle Registration Tax is the Irish government's answer to protecting the Irish car sales showroom industry, and a foolproof way of stopping every native who wants a new car from hopping on a ferry in Dublin and driving a nice new shiny one back from Liverpool, Manchester, or wherever. If any such car is to stay in Ireland more than one month, then it is subject to the VRT, unless you have owned the car for more than six months.

I bought our car from my old firm. It was my company car, and I made this purchase **one day** before we left. So, the extremely generous deal my former employers gave me, disappeared as in a puff of smoke, on the day I visited the VRT centre.

Well, nearly on the day. I sat in the waiting room while my car was inspected, only to be informed a few minutes later that they could not find my exact model on the VRT database, and that they would contact me within a week or so to tell me what I would have to pay to keep the car here. I had no idea how much this charge was going to be, until I received, by text, the following Monday, the more than a little disappointing news that I would have to fork out well over €3K to keep my car at my home. This was non-negotiable, my offer to sign a legally binding affidavit, that I would keep the car at least three years, fell on unhearing ears.

So, and this next bit is very Ireland, off I toddle back to the VRT centre, on the Friday of the same week, screaming Debit Card in hand. I present myself at the counter, gave them my reference number and say, "I've come to pay." To my utter astonishment, the nice lady behind the counter tells me there is an excess charge of €200 late payment fee to apply. At the same time she is saying this, she hands me a form in a most engaging way, saying, "That's where you can claim it back from." I of course want to ask her, if I can claim it back, why are you charging me in the first place, but I just know this would be a futile effort. She was very pleasant, but jobsworths are jobsworths in whatever country you come across them.

Of course the first thing I did when I got home was to fill in this damn form and send it off post haste; and to be fair, within a week I received a printed cheque back for the correct amount. It was quite bizarre that I should have to pay any excess anyway, as it wasn't my fault the payment was late, but as Linus Van Pelt liked to say, "You can't fight City Hall."

That wasn't quite the end of my Irish car-related horror show, I now needed Irish Car Insurance.

You can always tell if someone is from the Irish car insurance business. They usually ride a horse, wear a mask, and point a pistol at you. I arrived with a letter from the insurance company, who had provided the cover for my company car for a great number of years. The letter told of a claim-free record;

not one single penny had my company claimed on my behalf. The letter told of this dazzling achievement, to whomever it may concern. Well, where better to go than the same company on whose letter-headed paper I had such a glowing endorsement. You think? Didn't want to know. Not the slightest bit interested in their own company's affidavit. My company in the UK had been paying a little over £200 per annum, fully comp. Here the same company wanted €900+.

Somebody really should do something about it.

There is another aspect of motoring in Ireland which will be attractive to the UK motorist. No Speed Cameras. I can't vouch that this is the case in Dublin, because I drive in the city as little possible; that said, I've never seen one.

This is a boon to me, because even though I've never considered myself to be a speedy driver, I did at one point, back in the UK, get to being on the brink of twelve points, which is never a good situation for a travelling salesman to be in. I hasten to add here that I have never been 'done' for anything excessive: all my points have been garnered for doing 30 odd mph in a 30 zone or 40 odd mph in a 40 zone, never more than ten miles over the limit. So how annoying it was to be caught yet again by a camera on a big wide, quiet thoroughfare to the east of Manchester. I caught a glimpse of the dreaded flash and saw to my horror no other car behind me – it was me.

And so it came to pass that, in time, through my South Yorkshire letter box, dropped the inevitable correspondence from the Greater Manchester Constabulary. I duly filled this in, returned it and waited for the inevitable response ... which never came!

"Still haven't heard anything," I'd say on a subsequent visit to Buxton. My solicitor friend advised that there was a six-month time moratorium on these tickets, and if I hadn't heard anything by mid-September, I should be in the clear. Someone's probably lost the paperwork, he offered.

Mid-September came and went, as did all of October; we had a laugh and a beer, and he told me I was a lucky so and so.

Then, in November, I received a summons to go to Court in Manchester; Ange and I were studying the paperwork sent by the court, and it was obvious that I was not being summonsed for the speeding offence, but for failing to respond to the paperwork they had sent me, following my return to them of the initial forms. Copies enclosed.

It was at this point that Ange donned her finest Miss Marple twin-set and pearls, and noticed what I hadn't, namely, the wrong post code on the previous summons, the one I hadn't replied to, because we had never seen it.

The new summons was to appear at court in the first week of January, so I naively thought that wouldn't happen, and we could clear up the mess beforehand. How wrong I was. My solicitor friend explained that my indictment, if that's the right word, would just sit in a great pile of other such documents, and would almost certainly not be allocated to a member of the prosecuting team and so not even looked at until, at the earliest, the night before going to court and possibly not until the prosecutor is having his or her porridge (no pun intended) at breakfast. "We will have to go to court," he said, "but don't worry, you won't need to bring an overnight bag and your jammies." What a wag he is.

So there I am, sat in Tameside Magistrate's Court, in what

looks like a work's canteen, obviously an area where legal teams can meet up with their clients and get a brew at the same time. The only other person in the room is a young lady who is obviously from the legal profession. I look around me and, as she looks up, I say, "Hard to imagine John Grisham being fired with inspiration by this place," she laughs but says nothing. At which point, my legal team/solicitor/friend arrives. We talk for a very short time before being ushered through to a waiting area outside the courtroom.

I'm standing in the dock, and I have to say, I would be lying to suggest not being a teensy-weensy bit apprehensive. I've done the bible bit. At which point my legal team/solicitor/friend stands up and asks if he may approach the bench. He beckons the female prosecutor to join him. I can't hear the chat that's going on, but my solicitor shows some papers to the lady prosecutor and then leaves them with the chap in the middle of the three on the bench; then both my man and the prosecuting lady sit down.

The chairman of the bench, for I guess that's what he is, looks at me and says, "Mr Knowles, would you be kind enough to tell the bench what your present address and post code is, and how long you have resided at that address."

I tell him in a loud and positive voice; he thanks me, turns to his right, and mumbles something to the man there then turns to his left and does the same, he looks up:

"Case dismissed."

That's it?

My legal team/solicitor/friend immediately stands and tells the bench that he will be claiming for his and my expenses; the Chairman, with a very quick nod to right then left, announces, "Granted."

So, that was the end of my battle with the forces of law and order; never before or since has my shadow darkened the courtrooms of this land, or any other.

I also got the £365 I had had to pay up front returned. *Happy Days!*

CHAPTER 12

IT CAN BE WET HERE

Ah, it's raining! The weather eh, what can one say? Well in all honesty it does rain a tad here. As I write this, and look out onto my patio, the rain is actually coming down sideways. It's just biblical. It's as though the wind is picking up Lough Ree and slinging it the hundred or so yards onto my house, but, as a very wise friend of mine once said, "There's no such thing as bad weather, just the wrong clothes."

We rented for a total of eighteen months, twelve in the original bungalow, and a further six in another. We decided after twelve months that we loved it here and put our house in Doncaster on the market. We had a piece of luck in that the people renting Doncaster wanted to buy it; so, in a very short time we were on the lookout for a property and in the healthy position of being cash buyers. The bungalow we now 'own' is perfect for us, with its view of river and lough.

We journeyed for business earlier this week, mostly through County Mayo, and though we had a beautiful cloudless day I couldn't help but think that the surface area of water on this island must be near double the norm at this springtime of year; there were so many flooded fields and swollen, burst rivers. Mayo, at the best of times, is one of the wettest, but most beautiful, counties in the republic, averaging in parts towards 100 inches of rain a year. Of course, much of this falls on the stunning mountains of that county but nevertheless, to use an old footballing phrase, the ground is 'taking a stud'. There's an old Irish saying that Lough Erne is in County Fermanagh but, after rain like we've had, County Fermanagh is in Lough Erne.

One result of the somewhat precipitous nature of the weather on this island could be highlighted perfectly if only I had a topographical map to hand, so let's just imagine the island etched as though a spider had webbed it, these lines would be the 70000+km of rivers that mesh the country. That is some distance! Stretched end to end, all the rivers, becks, babbling brooks, creeks, streams, and tributaries, would almost go around the equator twice ...

I mentioned when talking about our first holiday here just how impressive many of these rivers are, and there are so many. The mightiest of these splendid water courses is without doubt the majestic Shannon, which is flowing only yards from where I sit.

The Shannon is listed in most places as being 224 miles in length, though this has recently been challenged, as it is thought the original rising point, The Shannon Pot, in County Cavan, is now not it's birthplace, and it might actually rise further north, in Northern Ireland. Regardless of its parentage, it is a fine body of water, which many thousands of people holiday on every year. Our own little community of Lanesborough/Ballyleague offers these travellers a choice of two marinas and the facilities in which to rest, recuperate, refresh, and re-hydrate.

Some stretches of the Shannon are quite stunning and it

threads through and knits together four of the country's most impressive Loughs, L Allen, L Boderg our own L Ree and then the largest on the river, L Derg. Just through Lough Derg, the river is harnessed by the Ardnacrusha Hydroelectric Power Station, which in itself is a monument to the country's founding fathers. Built within seven years of independence, this installation cost a fifth of the new state's annual budget but is still operating as a major power generator today.

As with most significant rivers, the Shannon would historically have been the major conduit for both the movement of people and trade. So important was the river that it was joined to Dublin by not one but two canals: The Grand and The Royal. The last working barge passed through the Grand Canal as recently as 1960; and as the route of this waterway passed very close to St James's Gate, one can only guess that it was carrying black gold to beyond the pale.

I mentioned how beautiful and mountainous Co. Mayo is; perhaps its most famous peak is the Holy Mountain of St Patrick, known universally as Croagh Patrick. This is a stunning, conical peak that rises 2507 ft to the summit, and you see it all, because like so many Irish peaks, it comes almost straight out of the sea.

The last Sunday in July is known as Pilgrimage or Reek Sunday, and, on this day, Croagh Patrick is climbed every year by between fifteen and thirty thousand people, in one day! Imagine. It is a quite staggering sight. This I know, because on 30th July 2018 Ange took part in the pilgrimage, and climbed it.

I had a bad knee.

We were blessed with beautiful weather, and Ange said the view from the summit, over Clew Bay, was astonishing. She also said that the climb up was very challenging and arduous, and more than a little steep; however, this she said was nothing compared to the difficulty she experienced in descending the hill. A lot of the path is but loose scree, and without the obligatory walking staff, would have been nigh on impossible.

After eight hours or so, having managed to make contact with Ange by phone, I hobbled up the first few metres of the path and waited for her to appear. Sure enough, she soon arrived into view, arm in arm with a little, and seemingly frail, old lady. Ange introduced me to the lady, explaining that she was 82 and had 'done' Croagh Patrick over 40 times. I thanked her profusely for helping Ange down!

Driving back to Lanesborough, an exhausted though elated Ange left me in absolutely no doubt that once was going to be enough for her.

We went to the pub.

CHAPTER 13

HERE I SIT, BROKEN HEARTED

I'm not sure if I've succeeded, but one of the reasons for these jottings is to try and convey to people the reason, or reasons, that we love it here so much. What I hope it's not conveying, is that this place is so much better than the other. In many ways it's not: it's the differences that generate the interest; though I appreciate comparisons are inevitable.

I think one of the reasons we've so taken to this community is that we like to get involved. We know this has been a factor, because people tell us it has. We hadn't been here very long when Ange spotted that there was a Music and Poetry group that met every second Monday in our local library.

So, Music and Poetry, well let's face it, I have the voice of an angel and a propensity to the rhyming couplet that might make the Bard himself green with envy. Ah, 'perchance to dream', that was one of his. The reality is, of course, that I sing like a stone, and have never written or really indulged in poetry; but, and this feels like my coming out moment, I have always rather enjoyed it. *(That said, I did pen the few lines at the end of part two, and those at the end of the book, and with that you have my entire poetic oeuvre.)*

Now don't get me wrong here, I do not have bookshelves full of poetry, I do have The Best of Betjeman, and a compendium of Dorothy Parker's verse, but that's about it; though bit by bit my collection is growing.

I'm a bit conventional in that I like rhyme, and I like to laugh and/or be moved. Some poetry I really struggle with: it seems to me that what makes these highbrow poets, 'Poets', is that they try and say something simple, in the most convoluted and extraordinary way possible. Deep and dark; it's like a foreign language that you have to translate. Perhaps the way most people perceive opera. Well, that's me up against the wall; I doubt there is some corner of Westminster Abbey reserved for my kind.

So, we didn't really know what to expect as we visited the Library on that first Monday afternoon. Well, when I visited, Ange was already there; she had previously started attending the Knit and Chat (Needles and Tongues) group, and they meet every Monday. They sit around a square of tables, clicking away like trainee tricoteuses.

Poetry was absolutely a new experience for both Ange and me. It's something that had hardly breached the horizon for either of us. As previously mentioned, I did possess a Best of Betjeman, a man I became charmed with after his numerous Parkinson interviews. And as for Dorothy Parker, well I can't remember where, but I came across the following somewhere and was smitten immediately:

By the time you say you're his,
Shivering and sighing,
And he vows his passion is
Infinite, undying ---

Lady, make a note of this:

One of you is lying.

And anyone who can write the following is alright by me:

I like to have a Martini,

Two at the very most,

After three I'm under the table,

After four I'm under the host.

Dorothy Parker was a fascinating woman who, in my humble opinion, deserves to be remembered much better than she actually is, and I would encourage everyone to look her up and read some of the marvellous witty things she wrote.

In Hollywood, she was one of the main writers for the original version of *A Star is Born*, a film remade on a number of occasions, most recently starring Lady GaGa and Bradley Cooper.

One of Miss Parker's most cutting pieces of theatre criticism was reserved for Katherine Hepburn – "She ran the gamut of emotions, from A to B" – I'm not sure this makes Ms Parker a great theatre critic; just a funny lady.

It was the former of the above poems that I read out at one of the first meetings we attended, and I subsequently found a niche at our little gatherings for lightening the mood by way of other humorous verses. We have discovered that my voice has a natural northern timbre for reciting some of the hilarious Stanley Holloway monologues, which seem to go down well.

Our group can number between ten and fifteen on any given second Monday, and while you couldn't describe us as a young lot, you could most definitely describe us as experienced.

I think it's this aspect of the group that so fascinates Ange and myself. Often a poem will bring back a memory or recollection to one of our number, who will then regale us with this reflection. In fact, any odd detail from a poem might ignite a memory of a past experience, often far different from those of our own. For example, we've learned what it was like, within our own lifetime, to live without electricity. Can you imagine, fetch water from a well, and visit the local bonesetter.

Our little group is called Poetry and Music and the latter is provided by Mary and Paddy. You'd never guess they were Irish with those names. Mary is our keyboard player, and lugs along to each meeting one of those clever organs that is multifunctional. Paddy is the man on the Sax who will often look up and ask if he's in the correct key; asking me this is like asking a blind man to play darts.

Our little group is lead from the front by Margaret, who is both an accomplished and published poet. She directs us with a schoolmarmly charm and quality, and it is, as much as anything else, because of her help and encouragement that I am writing this book at all.

I must give a mention here to another member of our little group, who is also a blow-in, though one far longer established than we two. Laurence is a Glaswegian, and an exceptionally fine poet himself, who regularly recites some very fine verses indeed. Much of his self-penned verse is quite short, but he has that uncanny knack of conveying the sentiment he wants in a beautiful, pithy, and often quite humorous way. His poems are a delight, and he should really find a publisher.

What's more, Laurence looks like a poet. He has the
bearing of a man who really enjoyed the sixties, and the smile
of one who can remember them. He sits with flat cap rakishly
off to one side, and an elegant scarf flowing down to
corduroy trousers. He also tells fine tales, as well he might, he
is the only person I know that has an entry in the IMDb.
Laurence wrote and directed a number of short films for, I
think, the Scottish Children's Film Board, this was in the late
sixties and early seventies. A very interesting man.

It is evident that, unlike in the UK, well at least in the
schools I attended, poetry is taught, I won't say, *ad nauseum,* in
Irish schools, but it was obviously high on the curriculum. My
fellow group members seem to remember all the old poems
they learned in school, often reciting along, silently, as
another member reads one out. We are also astonished at the
memory some people have for poems; one of our lady
members will regularly recite a fifteen- to twenty-verse poem,
without any *aide memoire* whatsoever, probably something she
learned fifty years ago.

CHAPTER 14

THE HUB OF LEARNING

We have been to a number of functions at the library in the four years or so that we have been here, and it is of absolute credit to the library service that they put such effort in.

One event was put on by the local historical society and was a simple celebration of Lanesborough itself. For this event, the library was bedecked with old photographs of the town, reminding people of an earlier generation of shops and premises, and no doubt of childhood friends and acquaintances. I was asked to read a piece written by a lady who was reminiscing about the colourful doctor they had in our village, the village of her youth, late 20s early 30s.

I will quote just a little of what I read:

He was a brilliant doctor, but a most unorthodox one. He had married and then separated after only one night (The mind boggles — my words), *and his wife moved to another location about ten miles away, to the nearest town. He certainly must have been affected by this short sharp marital state, he was a complete eccentric with a withering tongue allied to a very clever brain ... He delivered babies for miles around, but if called out during the night hours gave vent to his intense displeasure, any poor woman in labour had this extra worry to contend with … He was of course* (of course? – my words) *very partial to strong beverages and, when under the influence, was at his most venomous … As children we were scared of him, he wore silk dressing gowns, usually of maroon shades and he would stand at the door of his General Supply Stores, twirling his moustache, and casting a shadow on that side of the street.*

The doctor isn't named in the piece, though I'm sure that's on record somewhere, but what a fantastic subject for another book – who knows.

Our most recent visit to the library – since Covid put an end to such events – other than for the usual reasons, was another celebratory occasion. This time, the two celebrants were former members of the Lanesborough Writers Group, from which our own small poetry group has evolved.

In 2011 this group published a book of their writings, both poetry and prose, under the title 'Kindlings'. I have a copy of this book, and I am astonished at the quality of the work within. A number of the contributors are still with us. Margaret and Mary to name but two, and other members who still attend our little group have lovely work within.

Two members of the original group are sadly no longer with us, and it was in memory of these two gentlemen that our most recent celebration took place. I knew neither man, so cannot give a personal opinion of them, though they were obviously much loved by the packed assembly gathered that afternoon to honour their memory. Their names were Jimmy Casey and John Killian, and what I can do, with permission from relatives, is print two of their poems from Kindlings.

YIN and YANG:

A sonnet by Jimmy Casey

Why do winters come so soon
And take us all so unawares
Yesterday there was no gloom
Nor sorrows sharp nor weighty cares
The swallows gathered two by two
And Autumn fields in splendour lay
Where wheat and oats and barley grew
And farmers gathered in their hay.
And summer that had gone before
With days of sunny pleasure full
Which are what youth and age adore
When days and nights are never dull.
Soon spring will come with living force,
Then for dark winter, no remorse.

ALONE

By John Killian

Alone I am in the kitchen
But of people I think a lot:
Of friends of a different lifestyle,
Old loves now long forgot.

If its fate, it says on the signpost,
The decision is yours right or wrong.
It's the lone curlew's cry on the mountain
Or the nightingale singing her song.

Advice that was disregarded
Games claimed won – but not.
Thoughts of a long-lost childhood.
Alone? But maybe I'm not.

To be fair, let me think of the blessings
When through clouds the sun it did shine
When the friends and companions were waiting
With a friendship that was only sublime.

Those are the ones I'll remember,
The names that I'll bring to the grave.
They gave me the will to keep going
When I know I got more than I gave.

What a wonderful sentiment that last line propounds: to be aware at the end of your days that you received more than you gave.

These two gentlemen, who were so fondly remembered on that afternoon in the library, were also keen participants in the thriving amateur dramatic scene in the area right through the 1960s.

Walking down to the pub afterwards, it struck both Ange and me that what we had just witnessed gave sense to the differences that are manifest in the two countries we have lived in. Separated by such a short stretch of water. It seemed to us, from different ends of the planet, when it comes to everyday culture and what actually matters to people.

CHAPTER 15

THE IRISH WAY OF DEATH

This brings me on to a more delicate matter, at least for those with quaint English sensibilities: this is the Irish way of death. Nothing could be more different from the way we mark such an occasion than that between our two experiences.

I know and understand that death is marked in various and, to us, odd ways throughout the world, but here it comes as quite a shock.

The first funeral we attended in Ireland was that of a friend and drinking acquaintance we had got to know in the local. He was a lovely guy, and nobody liked a song more than good old Fergie. It was through our friendship with Fergie that I became aware of that fine band, The Shannon Tones. Not exactly a band as such, but a CD of thirteen songs, all performed by local people. You quickly realise when you live here that there isn't anybody in Ireland who won't sing. This is by no means a dig, quite the opposite, we have nothing but admiration for them. Anyway, this band of thirteen local worthies each took on a well(ish) known song and made it their own. They produced this CD and it sold locally in such numbers that they raised in excess €10,000 for the very worthy charities of MS Ireland and Parkinsons Ireland. Fergie was one of the singers and gives a great rendition of the George Jones classic, 'He Stopped Loving Her Today'.

After the service in the packed church, and the funeral procession down to the graveyard, the Shannon Tones gave one final performance, as Fergie was laid to rest.

We've had two funerals in the last month.

Firstly, a cousin of Ange's from County Leitrim died, he had been poorly for a number of years and while this was less of a surprise than it might have been, it still came as a shock to the family.

To us, being some distance away, our experience here was very much an English one: we turned up at the church for the funeral in much the same way that we would have done back home. Only there must have been upwards of a thousand people in the church! It certainly seemed that many: never have I been in such a congregation.

Funerals are a lengthy service here, much more so, it seems to me, than back home, it's probably the Catholic sensibilities that I've never had, but it does seem to drag. There's more theatre here: grandchildren placing poignant memorabilia on coffin tops, and just at the time I thought it had gone on long enough, a best friend gets up to give a eulogy, which, I must say, was brilliant in the case of Ange's cousin, and our friend Fergie.

When the service is clearly finished, the entire congregation then passes by the close family members sat on the front pew, shaking hands and offering further commiserations. My god what a grind this must be for the family.

In Angie's cousin's case, a number of the congregation gathered at the graveyard as an Uillean Piper accompanied the coffin across and around the little pathways till it reached its final resting place. From the graveyard there are great views over the Leitrim countryside, and the town of Ballinamore, of which Ange's cousin was such a well-known inhabitant.

After this, soup and sandwiches in a local hotel, and a great chance for people to catch up with friends and relatives that only ever seem to meet at weddings and funerals. I guess that much at least is the same the whole world over.

I can, of course, only speak from my own personal experience here, but in my family back home in England, dead bodies were for close family only, if at all: and if a viewing was to take place, then, in my experience, it would always be a private matter at a funeral home. Apart from parents, I had visited the odd uncle, or aunt. By no means all of them, and I never felt under any kind of obligation to do so. Not that people are obliged to here, it's just the way it is.

We recently lost a very good friend: Paddy was one of the many people who welcomed us to this community with open arms of friendship. It was our wont to enjoy a small libation on a Saturday afternoon in Clarke's Bar, and Paddy would often come in to the pub at a similar time. He would always be smart, collar and tie, sports jacket, and always a kind word, "How ya settlin in?" I'd tell him and he'd say, "Grand, that's grand." He was a guy we both immediately took to and liked a lot.

I got to know him even better when we purchased our first property here; this was just over the Shannon and our nearest pub was now Rosie's Bar. This was also Paddy's closest pub, and it developed into quite a regular little session, for an hour or maybe two on a Friday teatime, for a small gang of us to chew the cud and enjoy a few glasses of porter, as Paddy loved to call the black stuff.

I learned of his Army career, a good number of years he served as a cook. When he came out of the forces, he cheffed at a number of local hotels and hostelries in and around Roscommon. He was a great family man, and proud as punch of all his kids and his lovely wife Bernie. A great man for a saying or two: if someone was waffling in the telling of a tale he'd let out, "Now either shit or get off the toilet", and many times I've heard him finish a small anecdote with, "If I had a pencil, I could write a book".

Paddy was diagnosed with a serious illness in the first week of January, but very sadly, as he was about to start his course of treatment, he contracted pneumonia and just didn't have the strength to fight it off. He died in the first week of March.

If I remember correctly, he died on a Thursday evening; word soon got round that the funeral would be on Monday, and the wake on Sunday, between the hours of 3.00-7.00 p.m. We were unsure what to do. I would have hated for people to think we were being disrespectful by not attending and, as Ange had said, showing her English discernment, she'd rather remember him alive than dead. However, we did go, and we were staggered.

It was only a short walk to Paddy and Bernie's house but as we walked down the alleyway that led onto their road, we couldn't help but notice how many people were about. Before their house came into view a long queue of people waiting to pay their respects had formed down the short drive and for some distance along the pavement; it was still growing as we reached the house. This whole scene was completely alien to me; never had I seen anything of the like, and the queue never seemed to get any shorter, for as a slow drift of people emerged from the back door to leave, just as many were joining the line behind us.

We slowly made our way towards the front door, and, as we arrived, we were given a little spray of hand-sanitiser. Coronavirus was a word that was just coming into the world's psyche but had yet to wreak the devastating effect that it was going to have on all of us.

In the parlour was Bernie and her family, I shook hands and mumbled some kind of lament. What do you say? and there was Paddy, resplendent and at peace, in his army uniform. A few more sad sighs and handshakes and we were through to the back door. A tent had been erected on the back lawn and was full of people who no doubt were sharing memories and recollections of the deceased.

As we made our way back past the seemingly endless and ever-growing snake of people, I couldn't help but think why; why would a society put a grieving family, at the lowest they're ever going to be, through all that? I couldn't see the catharsis in what was happening, it's not like that was the end of it; the poor family had to go through the whole damn funeral tomorrow.

We went to the pub.

Very strong winds and heavy, horizontal rain greeted us the next day. Rather than the sombre procession the occasion usually affords, people were rushing into the church as though they couldn't wait to get there.

It came as no surprise to Ange and me that the church was rammed, absolutely. When the service finally got under way, there was standing room only at the back. Just behind where Ange and I sat were a keyboard player and a lady singer; then the priest who was conducting the service introduced himself as Paddy's first cousin. As I have said, I am not a Catholic, but as you can imagine, by association, I have been to a number of such services over the years. I always feel a little, sort of, embarrassed when everyone else in the church knows when to intone the Lord's name, or, without prompt, know when to reply to something the priest says; I just stand or sit there dumbstruck. Even worse, when everybody else in the church gets up to take communion and again I just sit there like some lowly heathen. Heigh ho!

At this service the lady soloist behind us sang a number of the prayers/hymns, or other incantations, in the most beautiful melodic voice. This was the first time I had come across such singing at a funeral, and whilst one can hardly say it added to the enjoyment, it made for a better, nicer service. I thought so anyway.

As I have already observed, Catholic services are too long. I needed to pee at one point, and it was fortuitous that the exit for the loo was close to where we were sat. I made my way out into the corridor, where there was a great fug of eye-watering, throat-clagging incense, some people had just lit the incense burners, and all being in the one place, the corridor smelled like a hippy commune.

As we exited the church to make our way to the graveyard, the weather if anything had got worse, and the five-minute drive needed the wipers at full tilt. Too windy for all but the strongest and most strategically held umbrellas, we made our way to the graveside where suddenly, though not completely, the rain eased, and the wind dropped a little, as if we were being given a little window in which to finish the proceedings. The coffin was met by a number of ex army colleagues, and drummers, and a bugler played Paddy in, and out.

We went to the pub.

CHAPTER 16

THEY DON'T TALK ABOUT CRICKET MUCH

You would have to travel around Ireland with your eyes shut not to realise the iron grip that sport, of all kinds, has on this island.

The GAA (Gaelic Athletic Association) had been founded at a meeting in Hayes' Hotel, in Thurles, County Tipperary, on Nov 1st 1884. The organisation was established to preserve and foster the games and athletic events that were unique to Ireland. However, the organisation was always overtly political; its foremost aim was to wean the Irish people away from what were termed 'garrison games' such as cricket, rugby, and tennis and to enjoy instead Gaelic football and hurling (interestingly, the Irish Rugby Football Union had been already formed, in 1879).

The games of Gaelic football and hurling are played by teams of fifteen on each side. The very first thing you notice, as a foreigner, and even before the whistle is blown, is that there are players from each team dispersed on both halves of the pitch. There are two ways to score points. The goalposts are similar to those used in rugby; the crossbar is slightly lower than in rugby and slightly higher than in association football. Like in association football the lower half is netted to make a conventional goal. If the ball is hit over the bar by foot/hand/fist or hurl, then you get one point. Into the net, i.e., under the bar, you score three points. The score is always shown as Goals/Points so you have to do the maths yourself. EG: A score might be Roscommon 6-11 Dublin 1-2. This would mean that Roscommon beat Dublin by 29-5.

Many games, and here I think Rugby is a perfect example, are easier to watch and understand if you've played the game yourself. GAA Football, for obvious reasons, bypassed me as a player, so to come to a new game at 60+ years of age has taken some getting used to. I am yet to pick up on the subtle nuances and deft sleight of hand movements that come naturally to those who have played or watched it all their lives, but slowly and surely I am getting there.

This understanding of a game in which I've not partaken is a little less problematic when it comes to the sport of Hurling.

If you look up Hurling on one those search engines it will tell you that this game is ancient, and goes back 4000 years. I'm struggling to come to terms with that figure. Newgrange, one of Ireland's oldest historical sites is 3,200 years old, which makes it older than the pyramids; that a game might be nearly a thousand years older than that seems mind boggling to say the least.

What it is, without doubt, is a game for nutters! It's bonkers! It is in fact another Irish tradition that would lend itself to the Game of Thrones franchise with ultimate ease. It is also incredibly fast and skilful and, as opposed to Gaelic football, to my uneducated eyes anyway, the skill is easier to see.

The name comes from the weapon! that is used, a flat chunk of wood that widens and curves at the end; this is a hurl, and generally anything from two to three feet in length. They let the goalie use a slightly larger hurl. The projectile, or ball, is called a sliotar, it has a cork centre and leather cover, like a cricket ball, though slightly smaller and the leather is softer. Nevertheless, the ball can be hit with fearsome power and speed; a top player can hit the ball accurately over 350 ft at speeds approaching 100mph.

The trophy that the Hurlers play for is the Liam MacCarthy cup, and the footballers play for the Sam Maguire Cup. Both finals take place in the spiritual home of the GAA which is Croke Park in Dublin. This is a splendid stadium that holds, and is regularly filled by, 82,300 souls.

The GAA, as an organisation, offers much more than just governance of its two main sports. Something I had never heard of before reading about the GAA was Poc Fada, but boy, would I have liked to have a go. It is the most wonderfully Irish concept of any sport I can imagine and has been going almost fifty years. All you have to do is hit a sliotar, with a hurl, over a mountain and back! The men's course is about 5km, and the record is 48 hits, or pucks, an average of about 104 metres per puck, which is no mean average, shot after shot.

The GAA are also responsible for the sport of Gaelic Handball. There are about 200 Handball Clubs in Ireland, and the sport is played under one of four codes.

For the last fifty years the GAA has emphasised its position of being a community-based organisation rather than simply a sporting one, with the introduction to the GAA family of Scór. Scór focuses on the more Irish traditions of song, dance, music, drama, and storytelling. I think, devised as an off-season activity for both young and old alike, it has grown over the years, but unfortunately not every club has the personnel to take on the numerous duties required to cover all the disciplines. It is something I would have loved to be involved in; if only I had any musical talent, could sing, act, dance or even story-tell, I'd be a shoo-in.

Ah! the Sport of Kings. That this is a fact is proven by one of the most ancient texts in the annals of Irish history, the *Togail Bruidne Da Derga,* which translates as Destruction of the Mansion of Da-Derga. In this fine text comes a description of chariot racing on the Curragh during the reign of the monarch *Conaire Mor,* sometime between 110BC and 60AD; so, quite old then.

There are other mentions of racing on the Curragh in the 7th Century. There are also very early indications of Beach Racing in Kerry, and documented accounts of Horse Matches in Galway, in the 1200s. In 1603 a Royal Warrant was issued, entitling the governor of Derry to hold fairs, and markets, at which horse races might be staged, and it has just got more and more popular ever since.

Today there are 26 racecourses on the island of Ireland. Two in the North and 24 in the Republic. There are more racecourses per head of population than in any other country. To put this into perspective; at a similar rate per head of population, the UK would have 255 racecourses as opposed to the 59 it actually has.

I've not seen all the racecourses in Ireland, but I have visited a lot and gambled at a few. I was actually enjoying the racing at Killarney, the most beautiful of Irish racecourses, on that most remarkable, and momentous day for English sport, namely Sunday 13th May 2012.

I think racecourses are nice places, whichever side of the water you are, and there are certainly some very beautiful spots in the UK; in fact, I would go as far to say that most are really pleasant. In Ireland, my favourite four, so far, are Killarney, Punchestown, Ballinrobe, and Gowran Park, but there really aren't any unpleasant ones. Galway isn't that attractive, but it does hold one of the best week's racing to be found in the entire calendar.

There is one racecourse in Ireland that's just a bit different from any other, and that is Laytown. This is a beach track, the only one where they race under the Rules of Racing. Laytown is a small resort about 30 miles north of Dublin on the County Meath coast; they race once a year in September. I'm told it's a memorable day out, but best not to go on your Tod.

I say on your Tod, a phrase I've used and been familiar with all my life, because a) I didn't know this was Cockney rhyming slang, nor b) did I know it has a racing derivation.

Tod Sloan was a very successful American jockey who had a rough start to his life. When he was only young, his mother died, and his father abandoned him. He came to the UK to race, but was ridiculed for his unconventional Western riding style, and it was always said that he was on his own. Hence, on your Tod Sloan, but in the usual Cockney fashion they missed off the last word, as in 'ampsteads, or barnet.

You will have noticed that less than very little has been said about what we English might call proper football, maybe another day.

That aside, I was once enjoying a small libation in Clarke's Bar when the conversation turned to soccer, a friend (Man U) turned to me and asked me who the best player I had ever seen was. To his surprise, and the other Man U supporters listening, I said that for many years the best player I had ever seen was George Best, and I'd been lucky enough to see him on a number of occasions. Mouths opened, jaws dropped, it's quite unusual here to say anything positive about any team you don't support.

"But," I said, people nodded, as though expecting a *but*, "Ange and I did go to the Etihad a couple of years ago, because I wanted to say I'd seen Messi." I continued, "And I must say he didn't disappoint, he is certainly some player."

I left it at that, but before long someone asked who I thought was the better player.

After some thought I said, "Well, Best was certainly greedy."

Before I could say any more, my friend responded. "Greedy? Nah, I'm not having that."

"Really?" I replied. "And how many Miss Worlds have you slept with?"

CHAPTER 17

"THERE WAS NOWHERE TO GO BUT EVERYWHERE." (JACK KEROUAC)

So, it's a bit cloudy and dull today, but with wife and small dog as company, let us take a walk around this place we have come to love.

We live on a very small estate that is situated just off the short road that leads down to the Ballyleague Marina. We have a bungalow; originally the whole of this small development, apartments below, bungalows above, was built as a holiday home complex. I think that at the time these properties were built, the Celtic Tiger was roaring the loudest; sadly, shortly after it became but a meow.

We can drop down to the marina or go up to the main road, so we'll go up and come back through the marina.

The main N63 Longford-Roscommon road doubles as the main street in Lanesborough/Ballyleague and lies across the top of our little estate. When reaching the main road, the first thing you notice is a striking thatched cottage on your right, which is attached to the now defunct Slieve Bawn Hotel.

Standing on the corner here and looking straight across the road you see a plaque set into a stone pillar that reads:

NOEL HENRY RAN 82 MILES
FROM THE GPO IN DUBLIN
TO THIS SPOT ON
THE 8TH APRIL 1968
IN 12 HOURS AND 7 MINUTES.
(Lough Ree Athletic Club 2001)

You should describe Noel Henry as one of the founding fathers of Irish Marathon and long-distance running, and he devoted much of his time to raising both awareness and funds for this cause. He worked at the bank in Lanesborough, when we had a bank that is. The run that is commemorated by the above was undertaken to raise funds for women Olympians. He himself missed out by only one place in representing Ireland at the 1960 Rome Olympics.

We take a right aiming for the bridge, and over into Lanesborough. However, Riley, our Jack Russell, is on auto pilot and after only a few paces is trying to drag us across the road. How embarrassing! Across the road is Rosie's Bar, one of the very finest establishments of its type in the town, and a place, it would seem, that Riley knows quite well.

You can just glimpse behind Rosie's Bar the remains of an unfinished castle; this was started but not completed in 1220 by Walter de Lacy, Lord of Meath. That wonderful, magnificent castle in Trim was Walter's main home; in comparison to that this would have been like the gardeners shed.

Though straining, in an attempt to pull us backwards, we force Riley to carry on, and very shortly we arrive at the bridge over the River Shannon.

A short history of our river-crossing tells us that the old Irish name for Lanesborough/Ballyleague, which is still displayed at any road entrance to our town, is *Beal Atha Liag,* which would translate as 'Mouth of the Ford of Stones'; so initially the river could be crossed here using boulders placed by nature.

The earliest record of a bridge being built was in 1000AD by Malachy, High King of Meath. This was built in conjunction with Cathal O'Connor, King of Connacht; a joint effort in an attempt to thwart those pesky Vikings.

Another bridge was erected in 1140AD this time by the High King of Ireland, no less, Turlough O'Connor. That's two Kingly O'Connors. Well, Ange was an O'Connor. I wonder where all the money went.

The next new bridge was erected in 1667, but only a few years later was left destroyed following action in the Jacobite war 1690-91. The river was then left unbridged for a number of years and crossings were made by way of a ferry.

This system ended in disaster on Lanesborough Fair day in 1702. The ferry carrying some 46 souls and their wares to sell at the Fair capsized and 35 people were drowned. This tragedy led to Parliament being petitioned for a new bridge, and in 1706 a stone bridge, 300 feet in length, 15 feet wide, with a 9-arch span was built.

The bridge we see today was finally completed in 1844 but even this bridge has gone through a number of changes, predominantly to allow for the flow of shipping. Initially it had a swivel arch, but the increase in traffic proved more than this could cope with. In 1975 the bridge was made into a fixed-span type, with the first span on the Western or

Ballyleague side being modified to a square, and this is the span all traffic on the river uses. In the centre of the bridge today is a demarcation stone which allows you to stand with one foot in Longford – Leinster – and the other in Roscommon – Connacht – and atop this stone is a sun-dial, which as I write today, is totally redundant.

We turn right immediately after the bridge, thus missing the main street for now. We pass over the town's main car park which was the site of another now long disappeared Castle. This castle was built by one Geofrey Meares in the 13th c. Known as Meares' Fort, it enabled the Normans to maintain control of the river crossing by way of the ford. It is said that the stone from this castle was used in the building of the first stone bridge.

The car park is situated at the back of our village hall which fronts onto the main road. We walk past the buildings of the Lough Ree Sub Aqua club and Lough Ree Rescue. These are adjacent to an excellent children's playground; all this is to our right. This trackway leads down to the little quay area. It has a slipway and small, sheltered harbour of a fashion; two dinghies and it's full, mind. It was from this quay that Ange and I set off in the episode, 'Avast ye swabs'.

The track now leads us to a five-bar gate, with a small gap to the side to allow for pedestrians; this in turn leads into what was a limestone quarry. There are two information boards here. One gives a history of the quarries and its working practices; another is a comprehensive information board about the varied flora that we may encounter as we progress. There is little left of the quarry these days, other than a few footings from long gone buildings. There are in fact two small quarry faces, and the second one comes into view, having walked only a few yards up the path that we now follow, into the wooded area.

The path continues to a fork. The left-hand fork takes you up and above a second, smaller quarry face, and onto the road that runs across the top. We stay on the lower path and take the longer walk through the woods.

Soon we are at another information sign, giving detailed information as to the flora and fauna we may well encounter as we journey on. These information signs are very useful: not only do they give information about the nature of the area; but the town imparts, through a number of other such signs dotted hither and thither, information regarding all historic or other interesting features.

We are now on the Callows, a word used throughout Ireland for an area next to a wetland that may seasonally flood. Well, it most certainly did this year; the Shannon reached a flood height during January and February that many locals hadn't seen before. Where we are walking now is evidence to this as the line of broken dead reeds, which indicates the level the water got to, is way inland of the path we are walking on. This walk through the woods would not have been possible without waders earlier in the year.

The information sign that we are now at suggests that Pine Marten might be seen. What a delight that would be. Though having made many circumnavigations of these woods, we've never seen hide nor hair of one.

We reach a stile over which is a sign that reads:
Welcome to RATHCLINE

Semi native Woodland and Recreation Area.

We are now in dense ancient woodland and the path meanders and drifts, twists and turns with the geography. Almost all the trees, both standing and fallen, are covered in a thick verdant moss which adds to the ancientness of the place. The atmosphere is always humid, and the ground is dotted with little diamonds of colour from one woodland plant or another; purples and yellows seem to be the most common.

Again, there are small information boards detailing some of the more interesting trees and bushes. These detail lifespan and uses etc., and give other snippets of information. A sign for the **Sessile Oak** tells me that the tallest oak tree in Ireland is in Co. Wicklow and is 37 metres high. A sign for a **Holly** tells me the spines on its leaves can act as lightning conductors, protecting both the tree and nearby objects; who knew? The wood of the **Spindle** tree is used for making skewers and toothpicks, as it can be sharpened to a point without breaking. The **Hazel** tree, cut into rods, was used by our most ancient ancestors, woven to create walls and provide shelter.

We continue our circular walk through the woods until we are nearly back at the start, but we take the now right fork that leads us up the track over the top of the second quarry, and up onto Rathcline Road.

Were we to turn right here, walk for a short way, and then take a further right turn, this would take us down to Rathcline Castle. This is a far more substantial ruin than the one over the bridge at Ballyleague and has considerable more history.

The original castle of Rathcline dates to the 9th century and was built by the O'Quinn clan. It was later fought for, and became the property of, the victorious O'Farrell clan. (O'Farrell is still a common name in the area.) Later those irksome Normans turned up, and it became one of their little *pied-a-terre.*

Following the restoration of the monarchy in 1660, King Charles II set about rewarding those who had remained loyal to the royalist cause. One such man was George Lane, who was the son of Sir Richard Lane of Tulsk, a town in Co Roscommon about 16 miles hence. The king granted more lands to George Lane, and his portfolio now included Rathcline Castle, and he set about restoring and upgrading it to its former glory. In 1676 George Lane was created 1st Viscount Lanesborough, as the village on the Longford side of the river, also part of his land portfolio, was now called.

George Lane died in 1683 and the lands and title, 2nd Viscount Lanesborough, passed to his son, James. The good work of the castle restoration did not last long, however. In 1690 it was badly damaged by canon fire, in the Williamite/Jacobite skirmishes; the same ones that destroyed the bridge. Williams's army, in pursuit of the retreating Jacobites, ruined not only the castle, but the towns St John's church. Shortly after this episode, James 2nd Viscount Lanesborough upped sticks and moved to London. There he built two properties, one in Golden Square, Westminster, and a second on Hyde Park Corner. This second building eventually became The Lanesborough Hotel, as it is still named, and is regarded as one of the very best and most expensive hotels in London.

We, however, turn left and walk down the gently sloping

road towards the main street. On our left are still the thick woods but these soon give way to panoramic views over the Lough and river.

Soon we arrive at the town's crossroads. The main road to Longford takes a left at these crossroads (a left turn for us would return us to the bridge) so, right turn for us takes us up the Ballymahon road, which is what we do.

Soon we reach an area of the village called The Green. This is a small estate of houses built by Bord na Mona in the early 1950s. This was to cater for the much-needed workforce required to develop the huge area of Bogland around and about. There were in fact three areas of housing development, 68 houses were built in Cloontuskert, 64 houses here on The Green, and a further 22 just a few kilometres down the Ballymahon road at Derraghaun. During the summer months, and before full mechanisation, as many as 800 people were employed in the practice of cutting turf.

Ange and I are obvious 'Blow Ins', having been here such a short time, but people say that when The Green was built, people from all over Ireland arrived looking for work, and the housing it offered. At this time, Lanesborough was a veritable Babel of differing accents and brogues.

At the edge of The Green is another information board that tells of one Jim Murray, who was the village Blacksmith for thirty years or more; right up to the tractor taking over from the horse. His forge was just below this spot, and the board informs us that Jim had driven three large metal spikes into a Chestnut tree that stood close by. Using these three spikes, he could fashion a straight length of iron into a circle to form a rim for a cartwheel.

Under a spreading chestnut-tree,
The village smithy stands;
The smith, a mighty man is he,
With large and sinewy hands;
And the muscles of his brawny arms
Are strong as iron bands.

Longfellow.

This verse of poetry is twice apt here as it is directly over the road from the aforementioned and superb library facility we have. We cross the road to the library side, and just a few metres further up is the Roman Catholic church of St Mary's; here we turn left.

Our walk now takes us down to meet the Longford Road, and shortly we are in the Townland of Barnacor, which is where the first property we rented is situated.

Townlands are not quite unique to Ireland; some of the Western Isles have a similar system. They are basically a division of the land and are often quite small. The Parish of Rathcline, in which this walk is taking place, covers an area of approximately 20 sq miles, but consists of 45 townlands. These would then become part of the Barony of Rathcline, a larger subdivision of a county. The Barony of Rathcline contains about 168 townlands. In Ireland as a whole there are 331 Baronies, which means that on average there are about 10 or 11 Baronies per County.

Next, we leave the Longford Road and soon find

ourselves passing over a small humpback bridge, under which, are the narrow-gauge bog railway lines that the many little trains pulling hoppers of peat travelled on to feed the (now closed) power station. Immediately to our right is the graveyard of Clonbonny; we are now already in the next designated townland.

You cannot help but notice how well kept the majority of Irish graveyards are. No matter what season, there always seems to be an abundance of fresh memorial flowers laid about. I don't think the Irish love their mammies and daddies any more than we English do, but they certainly look after them better once they're gone.

Immediately adjacent to the graveyard is the home of Rathcline GAA. They were not always called this; there is a custom in many GAA clubs to take the name of the parish they are situated in, or that of an historical figure, which might or might not have some local significance; often both might be combined to form the club's name. One of the earliest clubs to be formed in County Longford, Rathcline 'John Martins' were involved in an early sporting controversy.

John Martin by the way was a County Down Presbyterian Nationalist, he stood in a Longford election in 1870 as Honest John Martin but was subsequently transported to Van Diemen's Land.

On the way to an early County final, Rathcline John Martins beat Ardagh; their opponents made an objection claiming that Rathcline John Martins had played an ineligible Roscommon man named Pah Fallon.

Pah was produced and happily claimed he had never kicked a football in his life, though he did appear remarkably clean shaven … Surely not.

While we are on the subject, the other GAA team in the community are over the bridge in Roscommon: different county, different parish; and they rejoice in the name of St. Faithleach's.

I know what you just read but trust me, it is pronounced Fall-yuzz, St Fall-yuzz GAA.

Both of these clubs are an absolute credit to their community; and like many sports clubs the world over, they thrive and exist solely on the backs of a few dedicated and hard-working individuals for whom no effort is too much to ensure the clubs survival.

We continue our walk up the track, leaving the Rathcline GAA on our right. This is a proper tarmaced road, as there are a few isolated properties and farm buildings up the lane.

We love walking here, the hedgerows burst with life; there is always a harmonious accompaniment of bird song and more often than not, to our right, a field with three donkeys in it: inquisitive souls who, if they are near enough, will amble down to the gate and offer their not insubstantial noses for a scritch.

Today we will turn back here, but it is possible to carry on to where the lane meets the bog railway, transfer onto the tracks and walk up to the Kilnacarrow Bridge, over which the bog railway crosses the Shannon and into Co. Roscommon, affording splendid views of The Mountain and the bog-lands of that fair county.

We retrace our steps past the Rathcline GAA, and back onto the Longford Road, turning right to walk back into town.

Back at the crossroads, there are situated two of the three pubs the village boasts on this side of the river. On our immediate right is the Yacht Bar, known by all as Joes, diagonally opposite is the Swan Tavern, which I've never heard it called, this is known as Adie's after a previous owner, in fact the present landlord's father.

We cross over and turn right back down towards the bridge, only to be amused yet again by Riley as he point-blankedly refuses to walk past the third of these hostelries, namely Clarke's Bar; he pulls and tugs to the extent he nearly slips his collar; I've no idea where he gets these ideas from.

Further down the road, we come to St. Mary's Hall. In 1955 St Mary's Hall was bought by the local priest, and it still remains the property of the Diocese to which the church belongs. In 1959 the hall reopened as the Pillar Ballroom. The hall was refurbished yet again in the 1980s and in the 90s an extension to the eastern gable was completed. We've enjoyed a number of functions in the hall in the few short years we've been around, most notably a hilarious play put on by a local amateur dramatic society, of *Father Ted*, 'god it was fecking funny'.

From here we pass over the bridge again, and, to Riley's dismay, take the path down through the marina, and not the one past Rosie's Bar. The river on both banks here has been superbly developed, paved, and fenced, with a number of seats where anyone can gongoozle[3] to their hearts content.

After a hundred yards or so, the path takes a right turn, as the river here opens up into the expanse of the Lough. Here on our right is a municipal tennis court, and to the left the 32-

---

[3] There was once a canal cut through here too for barges etc. to have easy passage using the navigation.

berth floating, public marina of Ballyleague. It's great fun walking up the walkways, getting a closer look at some of the beautiful boats that moor here.

There is a much larger but private marina just a little further upstream, still on the Ballyleague side, which has the facility to berth 120 boats, has hardstanding for others, and does repairs.

From here it is just a matter of a few yards to home, and our little trip around Lanesborough is back to where we started from.

CHAPTER 18

COVID 'N ALL THAT

I write this just a couple of days after St Patrick's day 2021. This reminds us both that it is almost exactly a year since the dreaded word 'lockdown' became a part of the world's vocabulary.

On June 15th 2020, a Sunday, we were enjoying a small libation in Clarke's Bar discussing, amongst other things, the burgeoning fear of the spread of Coronavirus. The Irish government had already outlawed all St Patrick's day festivities for the coming week. To anybody reading this who isn't Irish, let me assure you this is a big deal. What is also a big deal here in Ireland, and happens at about the same time is, the Cheltenham Racing Festival. This too was at the forefront of many thoughts, as the UK government had not, as yet, gone into lockdown; this meant many thousands of Irishmen would be shoulder to shoulder with even more Englishmen, and no restrictions in place! This coupled with the fact that the UK government had the week before sanctioned a football match in Liverpool, attended by thousands of Spanish fans, coming from a country that was rife with the damn virus. What was going on? The consensus this side of the water was that there wasn't much joined up thinking. Then, the landlord received a phone call.

"That's it," he announced. "The pub will shut at midnight tonight, until further notice."

An announcement that the world was going to end wouldn't have garnered a sadder response than this one little sentence received. Reaction bounced off the walls of our little bar, 'bound to happen', 'inevitable', 'for f***s sake', there was nothing positive that anybody could say. Then, Ange leaned into me and said, "Be good for your diet."

We had a couple more and thought it only right and proper that we should go and commiserate with our friends over the bridge at Rosie's Bar.

"Heard the news?" echoed around the bar as we entere.

"'Fraid so," I replied, "let's hope it's not for too long, eh!"

But wishes are only granted in Fairy Tales.

So, here I sit, twelve months on, as dry as a Bedouin's flip-flop. We did have a brief summer hiatus during which pubs that served food could open. I have to admit, I did venture out on three or four occasions, but it wasn't the same.

We now wait for the jab, and it can't come quick enough...

CHAPTER 19

MAY THE ROAD RISE UP TO MEET YOU ...

Where to begin the end? What we earnestly hope is that this book has conveyed the reason why both Ange and I love this country; we hope to have done this by highlighting some of the differences between one society and the other, and we sincerely hope that this should not come across in any way as Brit/English/UK bashing. That is not and never has been the idea. I have always been and remain a fiercely proud Englishman. That Rugby shirt comes out at every opportunity, the Derbyshire County Cricket one would too, if any one here would recognise it.

There are of course fundamental differences, and always will be, but the main distinction between the two is, I think, a simple matter of scale. These differences are quite dramatic. If you consider area: that England alone is not quite twice the size of R.o.I, at 50,000 sq. miles to 27000 sq. Miles, but, in that piece of land, that isn't quite twice as big, England has to fit in eleven times more people. Roughly 55m to 5m. This, in a nutshell, is where the big cultural disparity is, conversely the fewer people there are the more of them you get to know, hence that very true adage, people are nicer here, that they are, is because they have more time and room for you.

That it is a beautiful country is a given, but what makes it so, well for us, as much as anything else, is its hills; and over here there is no shortage of them. Ironically, we live in what is undoubtedly the flattest part of the country, but hills are never far away from wherever you are in Ireland. Well over half of the counties in Ireland have hills over 2000feet, and it is this spreading of the largesse, so to speak, that is so attractive. In England, the Lake District has hosts of beautiful and spectacular peaks, but if you draw a line across the north of England to encompass Nth Yorks, the Lake District and above, this would contain almost all of the country's height. Derbyshire, the county of my birth, has two peaks over 2000ft, and Lancashire and Devon also have a single point that attains this elevation. Herefordshire shares the Black Mountain with Wales, but after this there is little of what we might call high ground; we are of course back to the question of scale again.

Water is synonymous with hills, and there are more than 12,000 natural lakes here. County Cavan alone, it is said, has a lake for each day of the year. Apart from the 224 miles of the Shannon, the island has three more rivers that clock in at over 100 miles, and another one that measures 99 miles. In addition to these, there are another thirteen at more than fifty miles in length.

Essentially, Ireland is a farm; what isn't a mountain, hill, bog, or area of population, is farmed. With these unfarmable bits removed, about two thirds of the country remains to produce vast quantities of Irish beef and milk; these two products alone account for about three quarters of all production. The more fertile, arable parts of the country produce barley, wheat, and potatoes.

Ireland being an island, it's perhaps not surprising that the vast majority of the population live in coastal towns. Of the ten largest towns in the Republic, only two are not on the coast directly. At number seven is Swords, which geographically is North Dublin, and within a gnat's pizzle of the coast. At number ten is the Meath county town of Navan, which in 2016 had a population of a little over 30,000. All the other smaller inland communities sit on the great green map, like so many farm buildings.

I could go on, though I fear I'm beginning to sound like an advert for Fáilte Ireland. But, you know what, I don't mind that one bit. I do hope anyone who reads this book, but has never been to Ireland, is encouraged to do so. I'll list just a few of the reasons why:

It really isn't very far.
You can fly, or sail – in the car!
You can bring the dogs.
You can walk the bogs.
The mountains are amazing.
The sun is always blazing…?
There's lots of rivers, loughs, and lakes.
Even better, there are no snakes.
If you like a beer, this place is for you;
Even more so, if you like two.
Miles and miles of empty sand,
From Malin Head, to Warren Strand.

From Warren Strand, to Ballycastle,
Wherever you go there'll be no hassle.
There's myths, and folklore, ancient history,
Castles and Keeps, and all that mystery.
There's no better place if you like a punt,
Or to fly a kite, box, or stunt.
If you like a holiday on the river,
We absolutely can deliver.
If all you want to do is fish,
Nowhere better can grant your wish.
You can't come once, you will be back,
Because of all these things, the best is the craic …

Printed in Great Britain
by Amazon

75585915R00139